D1373054

D1417741

THE
BEDTIME
TREASURY

This is a Parragon Publishing Book
This edition published in 2003
Parragon Publishing, Queen Street House, 4 Queen Street
Bath, BA1 1HE, UK

Printed in China
ISBN 0 75257 687 9

Illustrated by

Jeremy Bays, Natalie Bould, Lynn Breeze,
Anna Cattermole, Maureen Galvani, Mary Hall,
Virginia Margerison, Paula Martyr, Julia Oliver,
Martin Orme, Sara Silcock, Gillian Toft,
Charlie Ann Turner, Kerry Vaughan,
Jenny Williams and Kirsty Wilson

Jacket illustration by Diana Catchpole

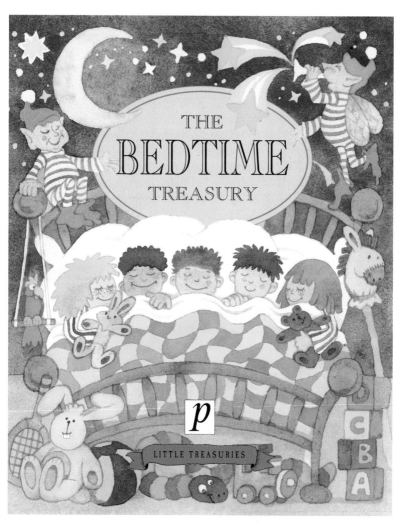

THE
BEDTIME
TREASURY

p

LITTLE TREASURIES

Written by
Derek Hall, Alison Morris and Louisa Somerville

Contents

Mr Mole Gets Lost

Mr Mole poked his little black nose out from one of his mole hills and took three great big sniffs of the air. "Oh dear," he thought, "it smells like it's going to rain."

Mr Mole didn't like the rain. His plush velvet fur coat got all wet and drippy, and he left muddy footprints all over his burrow. Worst of all, the rain got into his mole hills and then everything took days to dry out.

The skies darkened, and spots of rain began to fall. Before long, all you could see were long, straight rods of rain bouncing off the leaves on the trees, pounding the ground and turning everything muddy and wet.

Mr Mole wished the rain would stop. But it just kept on and on. It seeped into his burrow, it dripped through the mole hills, it became a little river of water. Then it became a bigger, faster-flowing river and suddenly Mr Mole was being washed along, turning this way and then that, as the water gushed and poured through his underground home.

The next thing he knew the rain water took him off down the meadow, not knowing which way up he was, through the woods at the bottom of the meadow, bouncing and turning him until he was dizzy and gasping for breath.

Suddenly, he came to a halt and he found himself stuck firmly in the branches of a bush. "Oh dear," Mr Mole said as he got himself free. "Goodness me, where can I be?" he thought. Being a very short-sighted mole – as most moles are – he couldn't make out any of the places that were familiar to him. He was completely lost and far from home. He couldn't smell any smells that were familiar to him and, to make things worse, it was starting to get dark.

"Woo-oo-oo-oo-oo!" said a voice suddenly. When Mr Mole looked up he found himself face to face with an enormous owl. "I wouldn't stay here if I were you. It's not safe in the woods at night" said the owl. "There are all sorts of nasty creatures that you won't want to meet."

"Oh dear!" said Mr Mole. He told the owl of his terrible watery journey and how he didn't know how to get back home again.

"You need to talk to Polly Pigeon," said the owl. "She is a homing pigeon who lives near your meadow; we will have to find her. Stay close to me, mind, and look out for those snakes, foxes, and weasels I told you about."

Through the dark, dangerous woods they went. Every now and again, there would be an unfriendly noise, such as a deep growl or a hiss, but Mr Mole didn't want to think about that too much, so he just made sure that he never lost sight of the owl.

Finally, just when Mr Mole felt he couldn't go on, they came to a halt by an old elm tree.

"Hallo-oooo," called the owl.

They were in luck. Polly Pigeon was waking up, and they found her just in time for she was about to continue her journey home.

"I'm afraid I'm terribly lost. Will you take me back to my meadow?" asked Mr Mole.

After a rest Mr Mole trudged wearily back to his meadow, following Polly Pigeon. As the sun lit the morning sky, Mr Mole smelled a very familiar smell – he was almost home!

His burrow was so wet and muddy he had to build some new tunnels higher up the meadow so that the rain wouldn't wash down into them so easily. Then he settled down to eat one of his supplies of worms, and fell into a deep, well-earned slumber.

Granny Casts a Spell

Susie was very fond of her Granny. Each day Granny sat by the fire knitting. Sometimes she knitted so fast that the knitting needles seemed to spark in the firelight.

"Do you know," Granny would say, "that I'm really a witch?" and Susie always laughed. With her smiling face and kind eyes Granny didn't look like a witch. Susie would peek inside Granny's wardrobe looking for a witch's hat or broomstick – but she never found one.

"I don't believe you're a witch," said Susie.

"I am," replied Granny, "and I'll cast a spell one day and my needles will start to knit by themselves." Susie kept a careful watch over Granny's needles, but they always lay quite still in the basket of knitting.

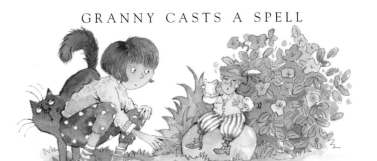

One day Susie was playing in her garden
when she heard someone weeping. It seemed
to be coming from an old tree. As she walked
towards the tree it got louder, but she could
not see anyone. Then at her feet she saw a
tiny little man, neatly dressed in a yellow
waistcoat and knickerbockers with beautiful
shiny shoes, and a three-cornered hat. When
the little man saw Susie, he stopped crying
and dabbed his eyes with a lace handkerchief.

"Whatever can the matter be?" asked Susie.

"Oh dear me!" sobbed the little man, "I am
the fairy princess's tailor. She has asked me to
make her a lovely gown for the May Ball
tonight, but a wicked elf has played a trick

on me and turned all my fine gossamer fabric into bats' wings. I shan't be able to make the princess's gown and she will be very angry with me." He started to cry again.

"Don't cry!" said Susie. "I'm sure I can help. My Granny's got lots of odds and ends. I'm sure she won't mind sparing some – after all, you won't need much. Wait here," said Susie, "while I run indoors and see." She ran up the garden path and in through the back door.

"Granny, Granny!" she called. In the sitting room Granny sat by the fire with her eyes closed, whispering to herself. Her knitting was on her lap – and the needles were moving all by themselves, so that the yarn danced up and down on the old lady's knees.

For a moment, Susie was too astounded to move. Then she thought, "I hope Granny's not casting a bad spell."

She ran back to find the tailor sitting in the middle of a pile of gorgeous gossamer.

"Where did this wonderful material come from? I closed my eyes for a moment and then there it was!"

"I don't know, but I think my Granny might have something to do with it," said Susie

"I'll never be able to thank her enough," said the tailor. "I shall make the princess the finest gown in the whole of fairyland. The prettiest dress there ever was. It was you who helped me in the first place. I would like it very much if you came to the May Ball, too."

"Thank you so much," Susie replied, "I should like that very much." But she knew she couldn't go – she was far too big to go to a fairy ball!

"Well I must get sewing," said the little man, reaching for a pair of fairy scissors. "See you tonight!" And with that he vanished.

Susie went indoors. Granny was knitting by the fire as usual and everything seemed so normal. Really, how could she have imagined Granny had cast a spell!

That night, Susie lay in bed and wondered if the fairies really were having a ball. In the middle of the night she awoke with a start. She could hear a click, clicking noise at the end of her bed.

"Granny is that you?" called Susie.

"Yes, dear," replied Granny. "I couldn't sleep, so I started knitting. When the needles started to twitch I knew it was time to cast a spell. What is your wish, Susie?"

"I want to go to the May Ball," Susie blurted.

With that Susie felt herself shrinking and looking down, she saw a beautiful gown, tiny satin slippers and gossamer wings. She floated out through the window and off to the Ball.

The next morning, Susie woke up in her bed. Had it all been a dream – the revelry, the fairy food, the frog band, the dance with the fairy prince? Then she saw something peeping out from under her pillow. And what do you think it was? It was a tiny, tiny shred of the finest gossamer fabric.

The Frog Prince

There was once a king who had one daughter.
Being his only child, she wanted for nothing.
But the princess was lonely. "How I wish I had
someone to play with," she sighed.

The princess's favorite toy was a beautiful
golden ball that she played with in the palace
garden. When she threw the ball up in the air,
it seemed to touch the clouds before landing
in the princess's hands again.

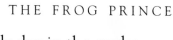

One windy day in the garden the princess threw her golden ball into the air and it was blown into the fishpond. To her dismay the ball sank right to the bottom.

"Whatever shall I do now? I have lost my favorite toy." She sat down by the pond and cried.

All at once a large green frog landed on the grass beside her. "Eeeuugh! Go away you nasty thing!" screamed the princess.

To her dismay, the frog spoke to her. "I heard you crying," he said in a gentle voice, "and I wondered what the matter was. Can I help you in any way?"

"Why, yes!" exclaimed the surprised princess, "My ball has sunk to the bottom of the pond. Would you fish it out for me?"

"Of course I will," replied the frog. "But in return, what will you give me if I do?"

"You can have anything I possess, even my crown if you will find my ball," said the princess, she was so eager to get her toy back.

"I do not want your jewels, your clothes or your crown," replied the frog. "I would like to be your friend. I want to be with you in the palace, eat from your golden plate and sip from your golden cup. I want to sleep on a cushion made of silk next to your bed and I want you to kiss me goodnight before I go to sleep, too."

"I promise all you ask," said the girl, "if only you will find my golden ball."

The frog dived deep into the pond. When
he surfaced again he threw the ball on to the
grass beside the princess. She was so overjoyed
she forgot to thank the frog and her promise –
and ran all the way back to the palace.

When the king, the queen, and the princess
were having dinner that night, a courtier
approached the king and said, "Your majesty,
a frog at the door says the princess has
promised to share her dinner with him."

"Is this true?" demanded the king, turning
to the princess and looking rather angry.

"When a promise is made it must be kept, my girl," said the king. "You must ask the frog to dine with you."

The frog hopped into the great hall and with a leap he was up on the table beside her.

"You promised to let me eat from your golden plate," said the frog, tucking into the princess's food. Then to her horror the frog dipped his long tongue into her golden cup and drank every drop. "It's what you promised," he reminded her.

Eventually the frog yawned and said, "I feel quite sleepy. Please take me to your room."

"Do I have to?" the princess pleaded.

"Yes, you do," said the king sternly. "You made the frog a promise."

As they reached the bedroom door she said, "My bedroom's very warm. I'm sure you'd be more comfortable out here where it's cool."

But as she opened the bedroom door, the frog leaped from her hand onto her bed.

"You promised that I could sleep on a silk cushion next to your bed," said the frog.

"Yes, yes, of course," said the princess.

The frog jumped on to the cushion and looked as though he was going to sleep.

"Good," thought the princess, "he's forgotten about my final promise."

"What about my kiss?" said the frog.

"Oh, woe is me," thought the princess as she closed her eyes and pursed her lips towards the frog's cold and clammy face and kissed him.

"Open your eyes," said a voice that didn't sound a bit like the frog's. She opened her eyes and there was a prince.

"Thank you," said the prince. "You have broken a wicked witch's spell. She turned me into a frog and the spell could only be broken if a princess would eat with me, sleep beside me and kiss me."

When they told the king he was delighted. The prince and princess became the best of friends and she was never lonely again. He taught her to play football with the golden ball and she taught him to ride her pony. One day, many years later, they were married and had lots of children. And, do you know, their children were particularly good at leapfrog.

The Castle in the Clouds

There was once a family that lived in a village at the bottom of a mountain. At the top of the mountain was a great, gray granite castle. It was always shrouded in clouds and was known as the castle in the clouds. No-one in the village ever went near the castle.

There were seven children in this family. The youngest son was Sam. His pet cat Jess was his only possession – an excellent rat-catcher. Sam was most upset at the thought of leaving Jess behind when it was time for him to find work, but then he had an idea.

THE CASTLE IN THE CLOUDS

"I'll offer Jess's services at the castle in the clouds. They will need a good ratter, and I'm sure I can find work there, too," he thought.

His parents were dismayed at his plan, but they could not change his mind. So Sam set off for the castle with Jess at his side. Soon the road started to wind up through thick pine forests. It grew cold and misty. They suddenly found themselves up against a massive, gray stone wall. They followed the curve of the wall until they came to the castle door.

Sam went up to the door and banged on it. "Who goes there?" echoed an eerie voice. A face was eyeing Sam suspiciously from a high window.

"Wwwwould you be interested in employing my cat as a rat-catcher?" asked Sam.

The window slammed shut, but a moment later a hand beckoned him through the partly open castle door. Inside, Sam and Jess found themselves face-to-face with an old man. "Rat-catcher, did you say?" said the old man. "Very well, but she'd better do a good job or my master will punish us all!"

Sam sent Jess off to prove her worth while he asked the old man, who was the castle guard, if there might be any work for him, too.

"You can help out in the kitchens. It's hard work, mind!" the guard said.

What hard work it was in the kitchens! By midnight he was exhausted but he noticed Jess wasn't around. He set off in search of her. Down dark passages he went, up winding staircases, looking in every corner and behind every door, but there was no sign of her. He was wondering how he would ever find his way back to the kitchens, when he caught sight of Jess's green eyes shining like lanterns at the top of a rickety spiral staircase.

When he reached her, he found that she was sitting outside a door, listening to someone sobbing on the other side of the door. Sam knocked gently at the door.

"Who is it?" said a girl's voice.

"It's Sam, the kitchen boy," said Sam. "Please may I come in?".

"If only you could," sobbed the voice. "I'm Princess Rose. My uncle locked me in here so that he could steal the castle. Now I fear I shall never escape!"

29

Sam pushed at the door. "Don't worry," he said, "We'll get you out of here."

He knew exactly what to do. He had spotted a pair of keys hanging on a nail in the rafters high above the old caretaker's head.

Sam and Jess made their way to the guard's room to find him asleep in his chair below the keys! Jess leaped up and climbed until she reached the rafters. She took the keys in her jaws, but as she jumped down a jug went crashing to the floor. The guard woke and caught sight of the tip of Jess's tail as she made a dash for the door.

The guard chased after them. "You go a different way," hissed Sam, and the old man disappeared after Jess. Sam put one of the keys in the lock. It fitted! He turned the key and opened the door. There stood the loveliest girl he had ever seen. The princess ran towards him, as he cried, "Quick! There's not a moment to lose."

Taking her hand he led her out of the tower.

"Give me the keys," she said and took him down to the cellars. The second key fitted the lock of a small cupboard. Inside was a golden casket filled with precious jewels. "My casket, stolen by my uncle," cried Rose.

The pair ran with the casket to the stables and saddled a horse. Jess appeared with the guard still chasing him. He leaped on the back of the horse behind the princess and Sam. "Off we go!" cried Sam.

And that was the last that they saw of the castle in the clouds. Sam married the princess and they all lived happily ever after.

The Boy Who Wished Too Much

There once was a young boy named Billy.
He was a lucky lad, he had parents who loved
him, plenty of friends and a room full of toys.
Behind his house was a rubbish tip. Billy had
been forbidden to go there by his mother, but it
looked such an exciting place to explore.

One day Billy saw a brass lamp
gleaming in the sunlight. Billy
knew the tale of Aladdin,
and he wondered if this lamp
could possibly be magic.
When his mother
wasn't looking he
scrambled up the tip
and snatched the
lamp from the top.

32

Billy ran to the garden shed. In the dark Billy could see the lamp glowing in his hands. He saw that the lamp was dirty and started to rub at the brass. There was a puff of smoke and the shed was filled with light and a man dressed in a costume richly embroidered with gold and jewels. "I am the genie of the lamp," he said. "Are you by any chance Aladdin?"

"N... n... no, I'm Billy," stammered Billy.

"How strange, I was told that the boy with the lamp was named Aladdin. But I may as well grant you your three wishes."

Billy began to think hard. What would be the very best thing to wish for? He had an idea. "My first wish," he said, "is that I can have as many wishes as I want."

33

The genie looked surprised, but he smiled and said, "So be it!"

Billy could hardly believe his ears. He decided to start with a really big wish. "I wish I could have a purse that never runs out of money," he said.

Hey presto! In his hand was a purse with five coins in it. Without thanking the genie, Billy ran down the road to the shop. He bought a large bag of sweets and took one of the coins out of his purse to pay for it. He peeped inside the purse, and sure enough there were still five coins! Billy ran back to the garden shed but the genie had vanished. "That's not fair!" cried Billy, crossly. He rubbed the lamp furiously and the genie reappeared.

"Don't forget to share those sweets with your friends," he said. "What is your wish, Billy?"

Billy was very fond of sweet things. "I wish I had a house made of chocolate!" he said.

Immediately there was a house made entirely of rich, creamy chocolate. Billy broke off the door knocker and nibbled it. It was really delicious chocolate! Billy ate until

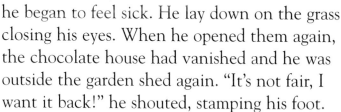

he began to feel sick. He lay down on the grass closing his eyes. When he opened them again, the chocolate house had vanished and he was outside the garden shed again. "It's not fair, I want it back!" he shouted, stamping his foot.

Billy went into the shed. "This time I'll ask for something that lasts longer," he thought, rubbing the lamp.

"You've got chocolate all round your mouth," said the genie disapprovingly. "What is your wish?"

"I wish I had a magic carpet to take me to faraway lands," said Billy. He was lifted up and out of the shed on a lovely soft carpet. It took Billy up and away over hills, mountains and seas to the end of the Earth. He saw camels in the desert, polar bears at the North Pole and whales far out at sea. Billy began to feel homesick and he asked the magic carpet to take him home. Soon he was back in his own garden again.

Billy was beginning to feel very powerful and important. He wished that he did not have to go to school – and so he didn't! He wished that he had a servant to clear up after him and a cook to make him special meals of sweet things. Billy became very fat and lazy.

THE BOY WHO WISHED TOO MUCH

His parents despaired at how spoiled he was and friends no longer came to play.

One morning, Billy woke up and burst into tears. "I'm so lonely and unhappy!" he wailed. He ran down to the garden shed, picked up the lamp and rubbed it.

"You don't look very happy," said the genie, with a concerned glance. "What is your wish?"

"I wish everything was back to normal," Billy said, "and I wish I could have no more wishes!"

"A wise choice! Goodbye, Billy!" said the genie and vanished. From then on everything was normal. His parents cared for him, he went to school and friends came to play. But Billy had learned his lesson. He never boasted again and he always shared his sweets and toys.

The Dog With No Voice

There once lived a prince whose words were pure poetry. He amused the court with his witty verse, yet he had kind words for all.

One day he met an old lady in the forest. He offered to help with the load on her back and soon they reached the old lady's door.

The old lady – who was really a witch – had listened intently to the prince. "What a fine voice he has!" she thought to herself. "I would like my own son to speak like that, maybe then he could find himself a wealthy wife and we'd be rich for ever more!"

"You must be thirsty," she said to the prince.
"Let me give you a drink." The prince drained
his drink to the last drop, but as he thanked
the witch he began to feel very peculiar.
He found he was getting smaller. He had
grown two hairy paws and a shaggy tail!
He tried to shout at the witch but all that
came out of his mouth was a loud bark!

The witch hugged herself for joy. "My spell
worked!" she cackled, and called her son.

A rough-looking young man appeared.
"What's going on, my dearest mother?" he said
in a voice that sounded familiar to the prince,
"and where did you find this poor little dog?"

"Whatever am I to do?" the Prince thought
miserably. "I can't return to the palace. They'll
never let a stray dog in." He trotted off
forlornly into the forest.

The witch and her son were delighted with
his new voice. He washed, then dressed in the
prince's clothes. "Now go and don't return
until you've found a rich girl to marry!" said
the witch.

He talked to passers-by. "What a very polite
young man!" and "What a wonderful way with
words," folk cried, to the son's delight.

The witch's son travelled until at last he
came to a castle where he spied a fair princess
sitting on her balcony. He called to her and

straight away she arose and looked down into the garden, enraptured by the sound of his beautiful voice. She guessed it must belong to a prince. Soon they were chatting away, and to his delight she agreed to marry him. "One with so beautiful a voice," she thought to herself, "must indeed be a fine young man."

Meanwhile, the poor dog-prince survived in the forest by foraging for roots and fruits in the undergrowth. He stopped to drink from a stream. As he dipped his long dog's tongue in the cool water, he caught sight of a pixie, fishing with a tiny net from a bridge.

"Cheer up!" said the little fellow, "I know how we can get your voice back. Follow me!" When they reached the castle the prince could see the witch's son in the garden calling to the princess on the balcony. She was so beautiful, he wished he could marry her himself.

"We will be married today, my fairest one" the witch's son was saying in the prince's voice. As the words 'my fairest one' floated up to the balcony, the pixie caught them in his net and gave them back to the dog-prince.

As soon as he had swallowed the words, the dog-prince could speak again. "Thank you, little pixie," he cried, "but what can I do? I am a dog with a prince's voice. The princess will never marry me."

"To break the witch's spell go to the church – now!" said the pixie and disappeared.

At the church the princess was looking most perplexed. "I don't understand," she cried, "I was to marry a silver–tongued young man, but now I find he is a dumb ragamuffin!"

"I can explain," exclaimed the dog-prince.

"What a handsome dog!" cried the Princess, bending down and kissing him on the nose. Immediately, the dog's hairy paws and shaggy tail disappeared and there stood the prince. "But you're... but he..." she stammered looking from the prince to the witch's son.

The prince explained and soon after he and the princess were married. As for the witch's son, he wasn't a bad young man, so the prince taught him to speak with a beautiful voice – and he married the princess's younger sister.

The Ugly Duckling

Once upon a time a mother duck laid a clutch of six beautiful little eggs. Strangely, the next day there was another egg that was much bigger than the others.

Soon the smaller eggs hatched into six pretty yellow ducklings. The mother duck sat on the large egg for another day and another night until eventually the egg cracked, and out tumbled a seventh duckling.

"You look different from my other chicks," exclaimed the mother duck, "you are big with scruffy gray feathers and large brown feet but never mind, I'm sure you've got a heart of gold." And she cuddled him to her with all the other ducklings. Sure enough, he was very sweet-natured and happily played alongside the other ducklings.

One day, the mother duck led her brood
down to the river. One by one they jumped
into the water but the big gray duckling could
swim faster and further than any of the others.
They were jealous and began to resent him.

"You're a big ugly duckling. You don't belong
here," they hissed as they chased him away.

The ugly duckling felt very sad as he fled
away across the fields. "I know I'm not fluffy
and golden like my brothers and sisters," he
said to himself. "I have scruffy gray feathers
and big brown feet, but I'm just as good as
they are – and I'm better at swimming!"

As he sat down under a bush he heard a terrible sound – CRACK! It was the noise of a gun. Men were out shooting ducks and, as he hid, a dog rushed past him, sniffing the ground. The ugly duckling did not dare to move until it was dark and he felt safe to come out.

He set off in the dark until eventually he saw a light shining. The light came from a cosy-looking cottage. The ugly duckling looked inside cautiously. He could see a fire burning in the hearth and sitting by the fire was an old woman with a hen and a cat.

"Come in, little duckling," said the old woman. The ugly duckling warmed himself by the fire, but when the old lady had gone to bed, the hen and the cat cornered him.

"Can you lay eggs or catch mice?" enquired the hen and the cat.

"No," replied the duckling.

"Well, you're no use then, are you?" they sneered, nastily.

The next day, the old woman scolded the duckling: "You've been here a whole day and not one egg! You're no use, are you?"

"I know when I'm not wanted," murmered the ugly duckling as he waddled off.

He wandered along until at last he reached a lake where he could live without anyone to bother him. Gradually the days got shorter and the nights longer. Winter came and the weather turned bitterly cold. The lake froze over and the ugly duckling shivered under the reeds at the lake's edge. He was desperately cold, hungry, and lonely, but he had nowhere else to go.

When spring came the weather got warmer.
"I think I'll go for a swim," thought the ugly
duckling as he felt the sun on his feathers.
The water was as clear as a mirror. He looked
at his reflection in the water and staring back
at him was a beautiful white bird with a long,
elegant neck. "I'm not an ugly duckling any
more," he said to himself, "but what am I?"

At that moment three big white birds just
like him landed on the lake. As they swam up
to him one of them said, "You are the most
handsome swan that we have ever seen.
Would you care to join us?"

"So *that's* what I am – I'm a swan," he thought. "Am I really a swan?" he asked, not quite believing it could be true.

"Of course you are!" replied the others. "Can't you see you're just like us?"

The ugly duckling, that was now a beautiful swan, swam across the lake with them and there they lived together. He knew that he was one of them and that he would never be lonely again.

Jimbo Comes Home

As Jimbo the circus elephant was snoring
away in his cage one night he heard a strange
noise. All at once Jimbo was wide awake –
his cage was on the move. Now this worried
him, because the circus never moved at night.
He could see men pulling on the tow bar at
the front of the cage. These were strangers –
it certainly wasn't Carlos his trainer!

Jimbo bellowed "Help! Stop thief!" But it
was too late. His cage was already rumbling
out of the circus ground and down the road.

When the cage passed through a gate marked *Zipper's Circus* Jimbo knew what had happened. His own circus family's greatest rivals, the Zipper family, had stolen him! But surely someone at Ronaldo's Circus must have heard them stealing him?

The next morning, the thieves opened up Jimbo's cage and tried to coax him out. After much struggling, they managed to pull him out. Jimbo took the biggest drink of water he could from a bucket and soaked his new keeper! When he appeared in the circus that night he made sure he got all the tricks wrong.

"Don't worry," said Mr Zipper to Jimbo's new trainer, "soon he'll forget that he was once part of Ronaldo's Circus." But Jimbo didn't forget. As you know, an elephant never forgets.

The other animals in Zipper's Circus had all been stolen from other circuses, too. "It's not so bad really," said one of the chimps to Jimbo. But Jimbo decided he was going to escape.

One night, a mouse passed by his cage. "Hello," called Jimbo. He was feeling very lonely and neglected.

"Hello!" said the mouse. "You're not very happy, let me help you," and off he scampered. Soon he was back with a bunch of keys that he had taken from the sleeping keeper.

Jimbo took the keys in his trunk and unlocked the door to the cage. He was free! "Thank you!" he called to the mouse, who was already scurrying away.

The thieves were snoring loudly in their caravan. Jimbo tiptoed up, as quietly as an elephant can tiptoe, slid into the harness at the front and began to pull the caravan.

Mr Ronaldo was dumbstruck to see Jimbo come home pulling a caravan just like a horse! Mr Ronaldo walked over to the caravan and was astonished to see the robbers still fast asleep. He raced to the telephone and called the police. The police siren woke the robbers and as they emerged from the caravan they were arrested on the spot and taken off to jail.

Mr Ronaldo, and Jimbo's keeper Carlos, were both delighted to see Jimbo back home again. They started whispering to each other and then walked away looking secretive.

"We'll be back soon, we promise," they said to Jimbo. They returned pushing Jimbo's old cage, freshly painted, with clean, sweet-smelling straw inside, and best of all, no lock on the door! "Now you can come and go as you please," said Carlos.

And Jimbo trumpeted long and loud with his trunk held high, which Carlos knew was his way of saying, "THANK YOU!"

Esmerelda the Rag Doll

At the back of the toy cupboard on a dusty shelf Esmerelda the rag doll lay on her back, as she had done for a very long time. It seemed to Esmerelda that it was many years since she had been out in the playroom with the other toys. Her lovely yellow hair was tangled and her beautiful blue dress was creased, torn, and faded. Clara always played with the newer toys at the front of the cupboard. Every time Clara put her toys back in the cupboard, Esmerelda felt herself being pushed further towards the back. It was very uncomfortable indeed.

Esmerelda could feel herself being pushed towards a hole in the back of the cupboard. She felt a mixture of excitement and fright at the thought of falling through it. One-eyed Ted had fallen through ages ago and never been heard of again.

One day Clara's mother said, "Clara, today you must tidy up the toy cupboard and clear out all those toys you no longer want."

Esmerelda could see Clara's small hands reaching into the cupboard. She couldn't bear the thought of being picked up and thrown away. "There's only one thing to do," she said to herself. She wriggled towards the hole and jumped. Esmerelda fell, and then landed with a bump on something soft.

"Watch out, my dear!" said a familiar voice from underneath her. Esmerelda had landed on One-eyed Ted!

The two toys were overjoyed to see each other. "What shall we do now?" cried Esmerelda.

"I have an idea," said Ted. "There's a rusty old toy car over there but I can't drive with only one eye. What do you think?"

"Yes, yes!" exclaimed Esmerelda, climbing into the driver's seat.

By now One-eyed Ted had found the key and was winding up the car. "Away we go!" he called as they sped off.

"Where are we going?" shouted Esmerelda.

"To the seaside," replied Ted.

They came across a black cat. "Excuse me," called Ted, "which is the way to the seaside?"

Now, cats hate water. "Why do they want to go near water?" thought the cat. "It's the other side of that mountain," he growled.

On sped the rusty car, up the mountainside. When they reached the top of the mountain they met a sheep. Now, sheep never listen properly. The silly sheep thought Esmerelda was asking where they could find a peach! "Down there," she bleated.

Esmerelda and Ted leaped back into the car and sped down to the valley below, but when they reached the orchard there was no sign of water, of course – just a lot of peach trees.

61

Just then a mole popped his head out of the earth. "Would you know how we can find the seaside?" asked Ted politely.

Now the mole was very wise, but very short sighted. He peered at Esmerelda's blue dress. "That patch of blue must surely be a river, and rivers run into the sea," he thought.

"Just follow that river," he said, and disappeared.

"We mustn't give up," said Ted. "We'll find it in the end." But soon the car spluttered and came to a complete halt at the side of the road. "What shall we do now?" cried Esmerelda.

"We'll just have to wait here and see what happens," said Ted. At long last they heard footsteps, and then Esmerelda felt herself being picked up.

"Look – it's a dear old tatty rag doll," said a voice. Esmerelda looked up and saw that she was being carried by a little girl.

Before long the toys found themselves on a windowsill in the little girl's bedroom. Esmerelda looked out of the window and nearly danced for joy. "Look Ted," she shouted. She could see the road from the window, and beyond that was a beach and then the sea. "We reached the seaside after all," she cried.

Esmerelda's hair was brushed and plaited and she was given a beautiful new dress. Ted had a new eye sewn on and could see properly again. The rusty car was painted and oiled. Most days the little girl took her new toys down to the beach to play with, and the days in the dark toy cupboard were soon forgotten. The little girl used to tell her friends the story of how she had found her three best toys lying beside the road one day.

Rapunzel

There once lived a man and his wife who longed for a child. At last their wish was granted and they were expecting a baby. Their house had a beautiful herb-filled garden but it was owned by a wicked witch, and they were scared to enter it.

One day, when the woman was standing by her window looking down into the garden, she saw a flower bed full of the prettiest rapunzel plants she had ever seen. Every day she would sit by her window, longing to eat some of the fresh rapunzel. Eventually she became quite pale and miserable.

"I must have some of that rapunzel," she said
to her husband, "or I may die."

The poor husband decided he had to do
something. Late that night he climbed the
high wall that surrounded the garden and
hastily snatched a bunch of rapunzel plants.

His wife was delighted. She made a salad of
them that was so delicious that the next day
she said to her husband, "I must have more of
that delicious rapunzel."

That night, when he dropped on to the grass
he found the witch there lying in wait for
him. "How dare you come into my garden
and steal my rapunzel plants," she shrieked.
"You'll live to regret this."

"Please have mercy on me," begged the man. "I came to help my wife, who is expecting our first child. She told me she would die if she didn't have some of your rapunzel to eat."

The witch changed her tune. "Please take as much as you like. But in exchange you must give me the baby when it is born. Don't worry – I will care for it as if I were its mother. What do you say?" The terrified man hastily agreed.

When a baby girl was born the witch came to take the child. Naming her Rapunzel, after the plants that had caused all the trouble, she took the child away with her.

Rapunzel grew very beautiful with long golden hair down to her waist. When she was twelve years old the witch took her to the middle of a forest and locked her away at the top of a tower. It only had one window at the top so that nobody but the witch could reach her.

The witch visited daily, calling out "Rapunzel, Rapunzel, let down your hair, that I may climb without a stair." The girl would wind her hair around a hook, lower it to the ground, and the witch would climb up. In this way, Rapunzel's lonely life went on for several years.

One day, a young prince riding in the forest heard Rapunzel singing to herself. He was so entranced that he followed the sound to the tower.

The prince found no-one and so he rode home, discouraged. But he returned day after day to hear her Rapunzel's singing.

One day the witch appeared and he heard her calling, "Rapunzel, Rapunzel, let down your hair, that I may climb without a stair," then a mass of golden hair tumbled down and the witch climbed up. "That is what I shall do." thought the prince, and the next evening he went to the tower and called, "Rapunzel, Rapunzel, let down your hair, that I may climb without a stair."

RAPUNZEL

The tresses fell down and the prince climbed up. Rapunzel was afraid when she saw the prince, but he addressed her in such a friendly way that she knew she could trust him. The prince said "I couldn't rest until I saw you. Now I cannot rest until you agree to marry me."

"You must bring some silk with you each time you visit. I shall weave a ladder of silk and then I will be able to escape," said Rapunzel.

The witch suspected nothing until one day Rapunzel forgot herself and said to the witch, "Why are you so much heavier to pull up than the prince?"

"You have deceived me!" screamed the witch. Snatching up a pair of scissors she cut off all Rapunzel's lovely hair. Then the witch drove Rapunzel from the tower and left her in a wild and desolate place to fend for herself as best she could.

That night, along came the prince to the tower, but the witch was lying in wait. She tied Rapunzel's hair to the window hook and let the golden tresses fall to the ground. But when the prince stepped in through the window he saw the witch. "Aha!" cried the witch, "you wanted to steal my girl, did you? She's gone and you'll never see her again."

Beside himself with grief, the prince threw himself from the tower, landing in the thick briars. The thorns pierced his eyes, blinding him. For many years he wandered through the wilderness looking for Rapunzel. Eventually, he wandered into the area where Rapunzel lived in miserable poverty.

Just as he had done so many years ago, the prince heard a sweet voice coming through the trees. He made his way towards the sound. Rapunzel saw him, recognized him and ran to the Prince, throwing her arms around him and weeping. As she wept tears of joy and sorrow, two teardrops fell into his eyes, healing them and restoring his sight.

Then the two were united again. The prince took Rapunzel back to his own kingdom, where they lived happily ever after with their children.

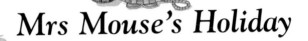

Mrs Mouse's Holiday

Mrs Mouse was very excited. All year she had been *so* busy, first gathering nuts and berries in readiness for winter, then giving her little house a big spring clean to make it fresh and tidy. Now she had promised herself a well-deserved holiday. But there was so much to do!

First she took out her little case and opened it, then she rushed to her cupboard and selected some fine holiday dresses. She chose several pairs of shoes, and a coat, some gloves

and a scarf (just in case it became
cold). Then, in case it became
very sunny, in went some
sunglasses, a couple of
sun hats some sun cream
and a sunshade. But, oh dear,
there were so many things in the case that it
refused to shut.

So everything came out of the case, and Mrs
Mouse scurried to the cupboard again and
chose an even bigger case. This time they all
fitted perfectly, and she shut the case with a
big sigh of relief.

Now she was ready. She sat on the train, with
her case on the rack above her head, munching
her hazelnut sandwiches and looking out of the
window. Finally, as the train chuffed around a
bend, she saw a great, deep blue sea
shimmering in the sun, with white gulls
soaring over the cliffs and headlands.

"I'm really looking forward to a nice, quiet
rest," she said to herself.

Her guest house was so close to the sea that she could smell the clean, salty air. "This is the life," she thought. "Nice and peaceful."

She put her clothes away then packed her beach bag ready for some peaceful sunbathing.

At the beach, she was soon fast asleep in a quiet spot. But a family of voles arrived on the beach, and they weren't trying to have a quiet time at all. The youngsters yelled at the tops of their voices, splashed water everywhere, and threw their ball at Mrs Mouse.

Just as Mrs Mouse thought it couldn't get any
noisier, along came a crowd of ferrets whose
noisy shouting and singing made Mrs Mouse's
head buzz.

Poor Mrs Mouse couldn't stand it any longer.
She saw a rock a little way out to sea. "If I
swim out to that rock," she thought, "surely
I will have some peace and quiet there." So off
she swam and was soon was fast asleep again.

Then the rock started to move slowly out to
sea! It wasn't really a rock at all, but a turtle.
Off into the sunset it went, with Mrs Mouse
dozing on its back, quite unaware of what
was happening.

MRS MOUSE'S HOLIDAY

As the turtle came to a deserted island Mrs Mouse woke up. She looked at the empty beach, jumped off the turtle and swam to the shore, thinking it was the beach that she had just left.

As the turtle swam off Mrs Mouse realized to her horror what had happened. But then she looked at the quiet, palm-fringed beach with no-one about but herself, and thought of the noisy beach she had just left.

"Well, perhaps this isn't such a bad place to spend a quiet holiday after all," she thought.

And so Mrs Mouse lazed on her own private beach with plenty of coconuts and fruits to eat and she made herself a cozy bed of palm leaves. But after a while she missed her own house in the woods and decided it was time to go home.

She took half a coconut, nibbled out the tasty inside and then found a palm leaf to stick in the bottom of the shell. She took her boat to the water's edge and she floated back to the boarding house to get her belongings.

Sailing back she thought, "This is the quietest holiday ever – I may come back!"

The Naughty Broom

"What a lot of dirt and dust there is on this kitchen floor," said the maid, who was very house-proud. Out came the broom from its place in the cupboard in the corner, and soon the maid was busily sweeping the floor.

Unfortunately, this kitchen had very tiny elves living in it and if you upset them they could be very mischievous indeed. The broom swept into a dark corner where the elves were having a party and suddenly the king elf was swept into the dustpan! The next thing he knew he was thrown on to the rubbish tip.

Coughing and spluttering with rage, the king elf climbed to the top. He picked the dirt and dust out of his ears and nose and tried to look as king-like as he could. "Whoever did this will be very, very sorry indeed," he shouted.

He made his way back to kitchen in the house. The elves looked at the king elf and did their best not to laugh. The king elf was still looking very dirty and untidy, but the other elves knew not to laugh at him because he was likely to cast a bad spell on them.

"The broom did it," chorused the elves.

"Right," said the king elf, "then I'm going to cast a bad spell on the broom."

The king elf marched over to the cupboard where the broom lived and jumped in through the keyhole. He shouted at the broom,

"Bubble, bubble, gubble, gubble,

Go and cause a lot of trouble!"

With that the broom suddenly stood to attention, its bristles quivering. Everyone in the house was asleep. The broom opened its cupboard door, unlocked the kitchen door and went straight to the rubbish tip. With a flick of its bristles it swept a huge pile of dirt, dust, bones and goodness knows what back to the kitchen. The broom then closed the door, took itself back to its cupboard and all was quiet until morning.

When the maid came down to the kitchen, she couldn't believe her eyes. She took the broom from the cupboard and swept all the rubbish back outside again.

The next night the same thing happened. Out of its cupboard came the broom, and into the house came all the rubbish again. There were fish heads, old bottles and all the soot from the fireplaces. The maid was speechless. She cleared up and then got the gardener to burn all the rubbish from the rubbish tip. But she still had no idea how it had happened.

THE NAUGHTY BROOM

That night, the naughty broom decided it
would make a different sort of mess, so the
broom flew up to the shelves and knocked all
the jars to the ground.

"Stop this AT ONCE!" demanded a voice.
The broom stopped its mischief.

"What do you think you are doing?" said the
voice again. The voice had come from a very
stern-looking fairy. She was a good fairy, who
had been imprisoned in a bottle by the elves.
The broom had broken the bottle and now
she was free. The spell was broken and it was
her turn to cast a spell – which she did:

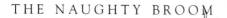

"Broom, broom, sweep this floor,
Make it cleaner than ever before.
Find the elves that cast your spell,
And sweep them off into the well."

The broom went to work. It swept so fast that
its bristles became a blur. Every bit of dirt and
dust, and all the broken bottles were swept into
the dustpan and out of the house. Then it came
back and swept all the elves down into the well.

The maid came down to a spotlessly clean
kitchen. She was puzzled to find some of the
jars missing, but it just meant that there were
fewer things to dust!

Little Red Riding Hood

There was once a little girl who was given a lovely, bright red cloak by her grandmother. She loved the coat very much, so much in fact that she never wanted to take it off. Because of this, she became known as Little Red Riding Hood.

One sunny morning, Little Red Riding Hood's mother asked her if she would take some cakes and apple juice to her grandmother, who was ill. The little girl loved her granny and was pleased to visit her.

"But don't delay," said Little Red Riding Hood's mother as she set off, "go straight to there and don't play in the forest on the way."

On the way Little Red Riding Hood met a wolf walking through the forest. Now Little Red Riding Hood did not know that he was wicked, and so she said, "Good morning, Mr Wolf."

"Well, good morning, Little Red Riding Hood," replied the wolf, "and where are you going?"

"I am going to visit my grandmother, who is ill in bed," said Little Red Riding Hood.

"Where does your grandmother live?" asked the wolf.

"She lives in the forest, not far from here," said Little Red Riding Hood. "Her house is easy to find. It's right next to the lake."

The reason that the wolf was asking questions was because he really wanted to gobble up Little Red Riding Hood and her grandmother. Suddenly he thought of a cunning plan. "Little Red Riding Hood," he said, "I have an idea! Why don't you pick some of those beautiful flowers which are growing in the forest and give them to your sick grandmother?"

"What a good idea," said Little Red Riding Hood. And with that, she set about picking a big bunch of the prettiest flowers she could find. In fact, she was so busy looking for flowers that she didn't see the crafty wolf skip away and make off towards her grandmother's house. The wolf soon came to the house, and knocked on the door.

"Who is it?" said Grandmother.

"It's me, Grandmother, Little Red Riding Hood," said the wolf.

"Come in, come in, my dear," said Grandmother, "the door isn't locked."

The wolf went into the house, saw the old lady, ran straight over to her and gobbled her up. Then he put on her nightdress and frilly night cap, jumped into her bed, and pulled the bed clothes up to his chin.

In a little while, Little Red Riding Hood came hurrying up the garden path. The door was open so she went inside and walked over to the bed.

Little Red Riding Hood couldn't see very much of her Grandmother, tucked up in bed.

"My, Grandmother, what big ears you have," she said.

"All the better to hear you with, my dear," said the wolf.

"My, Grandmother, what big eyes you have," said Little Red Riding Hood.

"All the better to see you with, my dear," said the wolf.

"My, Grandmother, what big teeth you have," said Little Red Riding Hood.

"All the better to eat you with, my dear," cried the wolf. And with that he jumped out of bed and gobbled her up.

The wolf felt very full and rather sleepy after he had eaten Little Red Riding Hood. After all, he'd eaten her grandmother, too. He soon fell asleep, snoring loudly.

Just then, a hunter passing the house heard the snoring. He looked through the window, and seeing the wolf lying in bed, he realized that the wolf must have eaten the old lady. While the wolf was still sleeping, the hunter cut open the wolf's stomach. To his great surprise, out popped Little Red Riding Hood and her grandmother. Luckily, the hunter had arrived just in time and both were still alive.

Little Red Riding Hood and her grandmother both thanked the hunter for saving them, and the hunter took the dead wolf's skin and went home.

Little Red Riding Hood's grandmother ate the cakes and drank the apple juice, and soon she was feeling much better. And Little Red Riding Hood? Well, she decided that she would never talk to a wolf again!

The Toys That Ran Away

"Put your toys away, Lucy," Lucy's mother called from the kitchen, "it's time to get ready for bed."

"Do I really have to?" she asked, knowing full well what the answer was going to be.

"Yes, of course you do," said her mother. "You should look after your toys properly."

Lucy never had been very good at looking after her toys. Once she left her new doll outside and she was ruined in the rain. Then she had dropped her tea set and some of the cups had broken.

And she was forever pushing all her toys in the cupboard. If she was in a temper, she would throw her toys in the cupboard, and sometimes she even kicked them.

Tonight Lucy was in another of her 'can't be bothered' moods. First she threw in some dolls, then the little tables and chairs from the doll's house. Lucy then picked up some puzzles and a skipping rope, and tossed them in too. Then she closed the cupboard door, squashing the toys even more, and went into the bathroom to have her bath.

Inside the toy cupboard Teddy said "I'm not going to stay here a moment longer."

"Nor me," said Katie the ragdoll.

"We aren't staying either," chimed the doll's house furniture.

All the toys agreed that they weren't going to stay. They decided they would all go back to Toyland and wait to be given to some children who would love them more.

The next morning when Lucy opened the toy cupboard, she couldn't believe her eyes. All the toys had vanished. The shelves were completely empty.

At first Lucy thought her mother had moved them, but her mother said she hadn't. All day, Lucy searched high and low for her missing toys, but they were nowhere to be found. She went to bed in tears that night, she was already missing them terribly.

That night, Lucy was woken by a noise in her bedroom. Was that a little fairy at the bottom of her bed? "Who are you?" asked Lucy.

"I have been sent to tell you that all your toys have run away back to Toyland because you treated them badly," replied the fairy

"Oh, I do miss my toys so much," cried Lucy.

"Well you had better come and tell them yourself," said the fairy.

With that, Lucy and the fairy flew out of the bedroom window, across fields and forests, until it became too misty to see anything.

Suddenly, they were floating down to earth, and Lucy found herself in the grounds of a huge fairytale castle with tall, pointed turrets and warm, yellow lights twinkling in the windows.

95

The fairy opened the red door and Lucy found herself in a large cosy room. In the corner was a kindly looking little man. "Hello," he said, "have you come to ask your toys to return?"

"Well... er... yes," said Lucy.

"It's up to them to decide, of course," said the little man. "They only come back here if they are mistreated. I repair them, then they go to other children who love them more."

"But I *do* love my toys," wept Lucy.

"Then tell them yourself," smiled the man.

He led Lucy into another room, and there were all her toys. Not only that, but they were all shiny and new again.

Lucy ran up to her toys. "Please, toys, come home again. I really do love you and miss you, and I promise I shall never mistreat you again," she cried, then she hugged all the other toys.

"Well, it's up to the toys now," said the little man. "Go back home with the fairy messenger and perhaps they will give you another chance."

Soon they were floating over her own garden again and through her bedroom window.

In the morning she awoke and rushed to the toy cupboard. There, neatly lined up on the shelves, were all her toys. Lucy was overjoyed. From that day on, she always treated her toys well and took great care of them.

Lucy never was quite sure whether the whole thing was a dream or not, but one thing really puzzled her. If it had just been a dream, why were all the toys so shiny and new again?

The Dragon Who
Was Scared of Flying

Once upon a time a dragon named Dennis
lived in a cave high up in the mountains with
all his family and friends. Now you would
think that Dennis would have been a very
happy dragon, but I'm sorry to say that Dennis
was, in fact, a very unhappy and lonely dragon.

This was because Dennis was scared of flying.
Dennis would stare out of his cave at his
departing friends, wishing he could join them!

He would stand on the ledge outside his cave, but as soon as he looked over the edge, he felt all giddy and had to step back. Then he would crawl back into his cave defeated.

The other dragons would return with amazing tales of what they had done that day. "I fought the wicked one-eyed giant and won," said one, "I rescued a damsel in distress," said another. "I helped light the fire for a witch's cauldron," announced a third.

"What have you been up to?" Dennis's sister Doreen used to ask him.

"Oh... um... this and that,"
Dennis would reply mournfully. He would try
again to fly, but the other dragons would laugh
so much that, in the end, he always gave up.

One day, Dennis could stand it no longer.
When the other dragons flew off to find
adventure, Dennis set off down the mountain
side. He had never been further from his cave
than the ledge, and soon he was puffing and
panting. He had to stop for a rest and his eye
was caught by something in the distance.
In the valley he could make out some brightly
coloured tents, and he could hear the strains of
music drifting up to him. "I'd better take a
closer look," thought Dennis. He got so excited
at the thought of his very own adventure that
he started to run. Then he got all out of breath
and had to stop altogether for a while.

At last Dennis reached the tents and found himself in a world more exotic than he could ever have imagined. There was a yellow, roaring creature and another one with stripes and fierce teeth. There were hairy creatures with long tails. Of course, Dennis had never seen a lion or a tiger or a chimpanzee before. They all stared and stood in a circle around Dennis, who stared back in amazement.

Dennis began to feel unhappy and unwanted again, but at that moment he heard a friendly voice saying, "Hello, there! Welcome to Chippy's Circus. I'm Claude the clown. How do you do?"

Dennis turned round and felt really confused, for standing there was a man with sad eyes and a mouth turned down so far that it seemed to touch his chin. Yet he spoke so cheerfully!

"I'm Dennis the dragon," said Dennis.

"A dragon, eh?" said Claude. "We've never had a dragon in the circus before. Would you like to join us?" he asked.

"Oh, yes please," cried Dennis.

Dennis was happy for the first time in his life. The other animals were friendly. Claude taught Dennis to ride the unicycle and to do acrobatic tricks, he learned how to dive into a bucket of water. He didn't mind that a bit because his slimy skin was quite waterproof! Now, as you know, dragons are particularly good at breathing fire and Dennis became a champion fire eater. Folk came from far away to see him shooting flames into the roof of the big top.

One evening Dennis was eating an ice-cream to cool his hot throat while Carlotta walked the tightrope. Suddenly she lost her footing and began to fall. Dennis dropped his ice-cream and flapped his wings furiously. He caught her gently on his back and flew down to the ground with her clinging on tightly. The crowd roared and burst into applause.

"Thank you, Dennis," whispered Carlotta in Dennis's ear. "You saved my life."

Dennis was overjoyed, he grinned and said "I do declare that flying is actually rather fun."

Mr Squirrel Won't Sleep

It was autumn, leaves were falling from the trees in the forest and all the animals began to get ready for winter.

One night Mr Fox came back from hunting and said to his wife, "There's not much food about now it's getting colder. We'd better start storing food for the winter."

"I'd love to go fishing," said Mr Bear, "but I'll have to wait until spring now." He went into his den, shut the door tight and sealed it.

"I'm off for a holiday in the sun, see you next year!" called Mrs Cuckoo as she flew south.

Mrs Mouse ran by with a mouthful of straw. "Must dash," she squeaked, "or my winter bed will never be finished in time." But soon she, too, was curled up with her tail wrapped around her for warmth.

Only Mr Squirrel wasn't ready for winter, he was leaping from branch to branch in his tree. "Ha, ha!" he boasted. "I don't have to get ready for winter. I have hidden a fine store of nuts, I've a beautiful bushy tail to keep me warm and I don't feel in the least bit sleepy."

The other animals all told him to go to sleep, but Mr Squirrel wouldn't. Not a bit of it. He danced up and down all the more and shouted, "I'm having SUCH FUN!" at the top of his voice.

Winter came. The wind whistled in the trees' bare branches, and it became bitterly cold. Then it started to snow. Mr Squirrel had a grand time making snowballs – but there was no–one around to join in and he began to feel rather lonely, cold, and hungry.

105

"No problem!" he said to himself and scampered down his tree to find his nut store. But the ground was deep with snow! He ran around trying to find his hiding places, but the forest looked the same in the snow and soon he was lost.

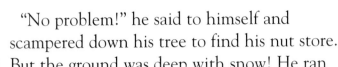

"Whatever shall I do?" He shivered with cold and hunger and his bushy tail was all wet and bedraggled.

All of a sudden he thought he heard a small voice. He realized that the voice was coming from under the snow. "Hurry up!" said the voice. "Dig a path to my door."

Mr Squirrel started digging frantically and sure enough there was a path and a door. Inside was a warm, cosy room with a roaring fire, and sitting by the fire was a tiny elf.

"I heard you running around up there and thought you might be in need of a bit of shelter," said the elf. "Come and warm yourself by the fire. I got lost in the

forest and when I found this place I decided to stay until spring but I don't know how I'll ever find my way home."

"If you hadn't taken me in I surely would have died," said Mr Squirrel. "I am indebted to you and if you will let me stay here until spring, I will help you find your way home."

"Please stay," replied the elf. "I'd be glad of the company." So Mr Squirrel settled down and soon he was fast asleep.

Days and nights passed, then one day the elf called out "The snow has melted, spring is coming. Wake up, Mr Squirrel." Mr Squirrel rubbed his eyes and looked out to see patches of blue in the sky.

"Climb on my back, I'm going to show you the world," Mr Squirrel said to the elf.

"Hold tight!" called Mr Squirrel as he climbed up through the branches to the very top of the highest tree.

The elf stared and stared. He had never seen anything like it in his whole life. Stretching in all directions, as far as the eye could see, were mountains, lakes, rivers, forests, and fields.

Suddenly the elf started to jump for joy.

"What is it?" said Mr Squirrel.

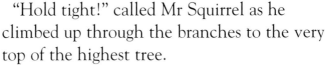

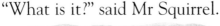

"I... I... can see my home," cried the elf, pointing down into the valley below the forest. "I must go home, Mr Squirrel. Thank you for showing me the world, I wouldn't have seen my home again without you."

When Mr Squirrel arrived back at his tree his friends were all very pleased to see him.

"I've been very foolish," said Mr Squireel, "but I've learned my lesson. Now let's have a party – I've got rather a lot of nuts that need eating up!"

So the animals celebrated spring with a fine feast. And Mr Squirrel vowed not to be silly again next winter.

Morag the Witch

Morag was a vain young witch who didn't know as much as she thought she did. She could turn people into frogs if they really deserved it, and do other simple spells like that, but she still had a lot to learn. The problem was Morag thought she was the most perfect little witch in the whole wide world.

Morag's adventure started when she enrolled on a course of advanced spell casting at the Wizard, Witch, and Warlock Institute of Magic. At the beginning of the day they were called in one by one to talk to Professor Fizzlestick.

"Now, young lady, I taught your parents," said the professor, "what kind of witch do you think you are going to be?"

"I'm better than my parents, and I'm probably better than you!" Morag blurted out.

"There is a truth spell in this room, so don't be surprised by your answers," said Professor Fizzlestick. "You appear to have a high opinion of yourself. What makes you so very good?"

"I'm clever," said Morag, "and I'm good, and I'm always right."

"And your dark side?" asked the Professor.

"I'm sorry to disappoint you," replied Morag quite seriously, "but I'm afraid I simply don't have a dark side."

"Well in that case I would like you to meet someone very close to you," said Professor Fizzlestick with a smile on his lips.

Morag looked to see on the sofa next to her… herself! As Morag stared open mouthed with astonishment, the professor explained that if, she had deceived herself, she was in for a few surprises.

As Morag and her dark side stood outside the professor's room, Morag's dark side jumped and whooped for joy. "At last," she cried, "I'm free. I don't have to sit and listen to you telling me what's right all day – in fact, I don't, I repeat **don't**, have to do anything that you tell me at all." And with that she rushed down the corridor, knocking over chairs and bumping into other little witches and wizards along the way. Morag chased after her dark side and finally caught up with her at the chocolate machine. "Don't eat all that chocolate," cried Morag. "You know it's bad for your teeth and will ruin your appetite for lunch!"

"Tsk!" scoffed her dark side. "You might not want any chocolate but I certainly do!"

Just then, the bell sounded for lunch. Morag wanted to find her dark side, but she also knew she mustn't disobey the lunch bell.

Morag sat down to lunch next to her friend, Topaz. She saw that Topaz was not eating her vegetables so Morag scolded Topaz for this, and gave her a lecture on eating healthily.

Topaz stared at Morag in amazement. "What has happened to you?" she asked.

Morag explained and said, "You know, it's the best thing that has happened to me. I was good before, but now I'm even better. I never want my dark side back, but we must find her and lock her up so she can't do any harm."

113

Topaz agreed, but secretly hoped that she and Morag would be reunited. Morag wasn't Morag without her dark side.

When she walked back into the classroom she discovered her dark side already there. She had already prepared a 'turning a nose into an elephant's trunk' spell was just finishing off a 'turning your teacher into stone' spell!

A trumpeting noise from the back of the classroom made Morag turn to find that the wizard twins, Denzil and Dorian Dillydally, had both sprouted huge grey trunks down to the ground where their noses had been. Morag's dark side was casting spells all over the place. "Oh, why doesn't the teacher stop her!" cried Morag to Topaz.

I'm sure you've guessed by now. Nice Miss Chuckle was entirely turned to stone from head to foot! Professor Fizzlestick walked into the classroom and Morag pointed to her dark side, still making spells.

"Lock her up," Morag begged the professor.

"I'm afraid that you are the only one who can do that," said the wise old man. "Without your dark side you would be unbearable and without you she is dreadful. Have I your permission to lock her back inside you?"

She agreed reluctantly and Morag felt… wonderful! It was so good to be to normal, to be good, but occasionally mischievous.

"Thank you," said Morag to the professor. "I think I've learned something valuable today."

"There is good and bad in everyone," he replied, "even the most perfect of witches."

Morag was so relieved to be normal. Morag and Topaz went back to the classroom to undo all the bad things Morag's dark side had done, but on the way they stopped at the chocolate machine first!

The Singing Bear

Long ago, there lived a young boy named Peter. He was a gentle lad who loved all creatures, but most of all he loved the animals and birds of the forest.

One day, the fair came to town and Peter was very excited. When it opened he tried the coconut shy, then he tried to climb the greasy pole and he used his last farthing on the tombola stall. As he was leaving he caught a glimpse of a dreadful sight. Lying in a cage, looking sad and forlorn, was a large brown bear called Lombard. He looked so dejected that Peter immediately vowed to set him free. The cage was strongly padlocked and Peter didn't know how he could break the lock. He turned to make his way home, with the bear gazing pitifully after him.

That night, Peter tossed and turned in his
bed. He wasn't strong enough to break into the
bear's cage and his keeper would surely not
agree to set him free. He resolved to get up
and go to the fairground to comfort the bear.

He slipped out of bed and made his way back
to the fairground. To his astonishment he
found the bear singing a song to himself in a
beautiful voice. Peter had an idea, he had seen
a piece of paper pinned to the palace gate.

"Lombard," he said. "I know a way to get you out of here. First you must teach me your song." Soon the two of them were singing the song together. Then Peter said, "I'll be back tomorrow. Remember, when you see me, be ready to sing your song."

Next day, Peter set off for the palace in his best clothes. Pinned to the gate was a notice: *The King Requires a Minstrel with a Fine Voice. Apply Within.*

Peter knocked at the gate. In a golden gallery minstrels were waiting to be auditioned. A courtier rang a bell for silence and in came the king and sat down at his great gold throne.

"Let the audition begin," cried the king. The first minstrel sang a song in a sweet, high voice that reduced the court to tears. The next sang in a deep, rich voice that sent shivers down the spine. The next minstrel sang a song so witty that the entire court laughed loudly.

At last it was Peter's turn. He stepped forward and said, "I beg your majesty's to allow me to perform my song out of doors, so that all the wild creatures of the forest might hear it."

"What a strange request!" said the king. However, he had grown quite sleepy listening to so many beautiful songs and thought the fresh air might liven him up. "Very well, but it had better be worth it!" he said, giving Peter a fierce look.

THE SINGING BEAR

"Follow me!" called Peter and led the king, the court and all the minstrels out of the palace gates and down the road.

Peter didn't stop until he was in view of Lombard's cage in the fairground. Lombard saw him and Peter winked at the bear.

The king's royal eyebrows rose higher and higher as he looked around him. "Well, I must say this is very odd indeed! We may as well hear your song. Proceed!" said the king.

Peter opened his mouth and mimed the words while Lombard sang. It was a most beautiful song and soon the king was sobbing tears of joy, mirth and sorrow all together.

"That was the finest song I ever heard," he said. "I would like you to be my minstrel."

"Sire," Peter said. "I wish I could accept, but in all honesty it was Lombard the bear who sang." Everyone gasped as they saw the caged bear.

The king looked furious, then he began to smile and said, "I admire your honesty, Peter, I would very much like Lombard to be my minstrel. Chancellor, bring me the royal purse."

Lombard was set free and became famous all over the land. From then on Peter went to the palace each day and sang duets with his friend, the bear. And it is said that, in the end, Peter married the king's daughter.

The Sad Clown

Bongo the clown had a problem. Clowns are supposed to be happy, funny, jolly people, but Bongo was a very sad clown.

Whenever the circus came to town people flocked to the big top hoping for an exciting day out. They thrilled to the performance of the highwire act, they enjoyed the jugglers, and delighted in seeing the beautiful white horses parading around the circus ring with the bareback riders balancing on their backs. There was always a big cheer from the crowd when the seals came on, for everyone loved them.

The biggest favorite of the crowd was the clown. Dressed in his big baggy pants he would enter the circus ring with his funny walk. They laughed when they saw his big floppy hat with the revolving flower on it. Even his painted clown face made them laugh.

Then his act started. First his bicycle fell apart, then he fell out of his motor car when the seat tipped up. By the time he had accidentally poured cold water down his pants and fallen into the custard filled swimming pool, the crowd were almost crying with laughter.

But beneath all the makeup, Bongo wasn't smiling. In fact, he saw nothing funny at all in bicycles that fell apart as you used them, or cars that tipped you out as you went along, having cold water poured down your pants, or even ending up in a swimming pool full of custard. He simply hadn't got a sense of humor.

All the other performers in the circus decided they would try and cheer the sad clown up.

"I know," said the high wire trapeze acrobat, "let's paint an even funnier face on him."

But Bongo still didn't laugh.

"Let's perform some of our tricks, just for him,"
said the seals. But Bongo still didn't laugh. In
fact, nothing that anyone tried made poor
Bongo smile. He was still a very sad clown.

Then Percival the ring master spoke. "I think
I know what the problem is," he said. "There is
nothing a clown likes better than playing
tricks on other clowns. If we find a second
clown, perhaps that would cheer Bongo up."

They hired another clown, called Piffle, and
the circus moved to the next town.

Bongo and Piffle performed their act. Piffle rode around on his bike while Bongo washed the car by throwing a bucket of water over it. Of course, the water went all over Piffle, who just happened to be cycling past at that moment. A smile flickered across Bongo's face at the sight of the soaking wet Piffle.

Then Bongo tripped while carrying two huge custard pies. Both landed right in Piffle's face. Bongo let out a huge chuckle of laughter when he saw Piffle's custard covered face.

THE SAD CLOWN

Then the clowns pretended to be decorators, painting up a ladder. Of course, the ladders fell down and all the pots of paint landed on the two clowns. Piffle had a big paint pot stuck on his head, with paint dripping down his body. Bongo roared with laughter. Piffle thought Bongo looked just as funny As for the crowd – well, they thought two clowns were funnier than one and they clapped and cheered and filled the big top with laughter. After that Bongo was never a sad clown again.

The Magic Tree

Tommy rubbed his eyes and looked out of his bedroom window again. There was an enormous oak tree that hadn't been there yesterday! If it had been there he would have climbed up it, for Tommy loved nothing better than climbing trees.

Tommy sat staring at the tree in wonder and disbelief. He wondered how on earth it had suddenly got there, but he decided that before he wondered about that too much, he had better go and climb it first. After all, there was always time later to wonder about things but never enough time to do things, he thought.

THE MAGIC TREE

He dressed and ran outside to take a closer
look. It seemed just like any other big oak tree
with wide, inviting branches, lots of green,
rounded leaves and deep, furrowed bark.

Tommy stepped on to the lowest branch and
up to the next – the tree seemed so easy to
climb. But something was not right. Branches
seemed to be so big that he could stand up on
them and walk in any direction, they seemed
just like trees themselves. In fact, he suddenly
realized that he wasn't any longer climbing a
tree, but standing in a whole forest of trees.

Tommy didn't like this at all, and decided to get down. But where was down? All he could see were tall, swaying trees and twisty paths leading off even deeper into the forest. Somehow got himself lost in a forest, and he hadn't even had breakfast yet!

"Quick, over here!" someone called out – the voice belonged to a squirrel.

"You can speak!" blurted out Tommy.

"Of course!" snapped the squirrel. "You are in great danger, and there's no time to lose if we are to save you from the clutches of the evil Wizard of the Woods."

The squirrel explained that the Wizard of the Woods ruled the forest, and lured people into his realm by making a tree appear. Once the tree was climbed, there was little chance of escape.

"But why does the Wizard of the Woods want to lure people into the forest?" asked Tommy, rather hoping that he didn't have to hear the answer.

"To turn them into fertilizer to make the trees grow," said the squirrel.

Tommy didn't really know what fertilizer was, but it sounded rather nasty. He was pleased when the squirrel suddenly said, "There is just one way to get you out of here. But we must hurry. Soon it will be dark and the Wizard of the Woods will awake. Once he awakes, he will smell your blood and he will capture you."

The squirrel jumped up the nearest tree and Tommy climbed after him. "Where are we going?" he panted as they climbed higher.

"To the top of the tallest tree in the forest," the squirrel answered.

"But why?" asked Tommy.

"Because that's the only way to escape. You'll see!" said the squirrel.

When they were at the top of the tallest tree they could see nothing but more trees. Tommy looked up, and at last he could see the clear, twilight sky. He also noticed that all the leaves at the top of the tallest tree were enormous.

"Quick," said the squirrel. "Sit on this leaf."

The squirrel whistled, and a hundred more squirrels joined them, each taking hold of the branch. With a great heave, they pulled and pulled until it was bent backwards. Suddenly they let go. With a "TWANG" Tommy and the leaf were launched into the air. They soared through the air until they began to float down to earth and landed with a bump.

When Tommy opened his eyes he was on his bedroom floor. The magic tree was nowhere to be seen. Perhaps it had never been there at all. Maybe it was just a dream. What do you think?

Bobby's Best Birthday Present

It was Bobby's birthday and he was very excited.
The breakfast table was covered with presents.
Bobby opened them one by one. There was a
beautiful book, a toy racing car and a baseball
cap. Bobby was very pleased with these, but
where was the present from his parents? "Close
your eyes!" said his mother. When he opened
his eyes there was a large rectangular parcel.
Bobby tore off the wrapping and inside the box
was a wonderful, shiny, electric train set.

It was so lovely he could hardly bear to touch it. Bobby carefully set up the track and soon he had the train whizzing round his bedroom floor. Freddie the cat came in and watched the train going round. When the train came past him again he swiped at it with his paw and derailed it. The engine and the six cars tumbled off the track and landed in a heap on the floor. "Look what you've done!" wailed Bobby. The cars were undamaged, but the engine had hit the side of his bed and was badly dented.

Bobby was very upset. "We can't take it back to the shop now, but we can take it to the toymender in the morning," said his mother. "I'm sure it'll look as good as new again." Bobby played with his other presents, but all he wanted to do was to play with his train set.

In the morning, the first thing Bobby did was to look at the poor broken engine. He couldn't believe his eyes. It was perfect! He ran to his parents. "Look, look!" he cried. They were as amazed as he was. The engine worked perfectly and Bobby played happily with his train set all day – but he made sure Freddie kept out of his room!

That night Bobby couldn't sleep. He heard a noise, it was the sound of his train set on the track. In the darkness he could definitely make out the shape of the train as it sped by. How had the train started? Had Freddie crept into his room and flicked the switch? Gradually his eyes became accustomed to the dark and Bobby could make out several shapes in the carriages. He could see that they were little folk wearing leafy costumes. "Elves!" thought Bobby.

At that moment one of the elves spotted Bobby. "Hello there!" he called. "We saw that your train set was broken. We wanted a ride so we fixed it. I hope you don't mind!" Bobby was too astounded to say anything at all. "Come with us for a ride," called the elf.

As the train passed him the elf leaned out of the car, grabbing Bobby by the hand. Bobby felt himself shrink as he flew through the air, and then he was sitting in the car of his very own train set! "Here we go – hold tight!" called the elf as the train left the track and went out through the window.

"Where would you like to go? asked the elf.

"Toyland!" replied Bobby. Sure enough, the train headed towards a track which curved up a mountain of pink and white sugar. There were all kinds of toys around – a rag doll with a shiny car, three teddy bears setting off for school and a brightly colored clown playing a drum.

"Now for some fun!" said one of the elves when the train stopped. They had come to a halt by a toy fairground. Bobby found that this was like no other fairground – all the rides were real and when he got in for the rocket ride, it took him to the moon and back!

"Time to go, Bobby," said one of the elves at last. Bobby climbed wearily back into the train. When he woke up it was morning and he was back in his bed. On a scrap of paper in tiny spidery writing, were the words: *We hope you enjoyed your trip to Toyland – the elves*.

Puss in Boots

Once upon a time in France, there lived a miller with three sons. When he died, the miller left the mill to his eldest son, and a donkey to carry the flour to his second son. But to the youngest son, who was much the most handsome of the three, he left only a large cat, whose job it had been to chase mice.

The poor youngest brother could see that he would have to go out into the world to seek his fortune. "I shall have to leave you behind, Puss," he said, "I won't be able to look after you."

"But I can look after *you*!" replied Puss. "With a drawstring bag and a pair of boots, I can make you a fortune," said the cat.

The lad decided it was worth letting the cat try, as he had no idea of what to do otherwise. With his brand new boots on his hind paws and his drawstring bag slung over his shoulder, Puss set off with a handful of corn from the mill.

He went straight to the rabbit warren where he put a little corn into the bag and laid it open near the rabbit hole. Puss waited until dusk for the rabbits to come out of their hole. A curious rabbit came up and hopped into the bag to get the corn. Puss pulled the drawstring tight and set off to the palace, where he announced that he had brought the king a present.

"Your majesty," said Puss, "I am a messenger from the Marquis of Carabas. He was lucky enough to catch a fine young rabbit today and begs that you will accept
it as a present."

The king had never heard of this Marquis, but he was pleased to have the rabbit. "Tell your master that I am delighted," he said.

Day after day, Puss went hunting and gave his catch to the king. After a while the cat started to be invited in for a chat with the guards and he soon got to know all the court gossip. Puss got to hear that the king was planning to drive in his grand carriage with his daughter, the most beautiful princess in France. Puss found out which direction they intended to take.

The next morning he said to his master, "I think it would be a good idea to take a swim in the river. Remember you're supposed to be a Marquis." Puss led the way to the river where the royal carriage would pass. While the boy was swimming Puss hid his master's clothes under a stone. When the carriage appeared he ran into the road shouting, "Help! The Marquis of Carabas is drowning!" The king recognized Puss and ordered his guards to go to the rescue.

Meanwhile, Puss bowed to the king and said, "While he was bathing, thieves stole my master's fine clothing. He cannot appear before your daughter without any clothes."

"Of course not," replied the king, and sent his footman for a spare set of clothes from the back of the carriage. The king was glad to meet the mysterious Marquis, of whom he had heard so much from Puss. "Come for a drive with us, my dear Marquis," said the king.

Without another word Puss disappeared and was soon a long way ahead of the carriage. Soon he passed a field of haymakers. "My good haymakers," said Puss, "you must tell the king that this meadow belongs to the Marquis of Carabas – or I'll grind you all to little pieces."

Puss knew that the meadow belonged to an ogre who could change his shape, so that no-one would know if he was an ordinary pussy cat – or if it really was the ogre. As the royal carriage passed by the king asked to whom the field belonged. "The Marquis of Carabas, your majesty," called the haymakers.

"That's a fine piece of land you've got there," said the king to the lad in the carriage.

Along the road it was the same story, Puss got there before the royal carriage. Everyone said that their master was the Marquis of Carabas. Then Puss caught sight of a fine castle which he knew belonged to the ogre.

Puss asked to speak to the ogre. Puss said "I heard that you can transform yourself into a lion. But I really can't believe that this is true."

The ogre was so offended that he bellowed, "JUST YOU WATCH!" and instantly turned himself into a lion. Then he turned back into an ogre. "That'll teach you," he roared.

"You gave me a dreadful fright," said Puss. "But you can't turn yourself into a tiny animal, such as rat or mouse. It's impossible."

"IMPOSSIBLE, EH?" screeched the ogre, and foolishly turned himself into a mouse.

Puss pounced on him and gobbled him up. Then the royal carriage rumbled over the drawbridge, for the king, too, had spotted the castle and wondered who lived there.

"Welcome to the castle of the Marquis of Carabas, your majesty," said Puss

"Is this yours, too?" cried the king. The lad nodded. "May we see inside?" asked the king.

The ogre's servants were so happy to be free of their master that they laid on a fine feast. Then at the end of the meal, the king agreed to give his daughter's hand in marriage to the 'Marquis'.

As for Puss, his master was so grateful that he saw to it that the cat was made a lord. So they all lived happily ever after and Puss never had to chase another mouse again.

The Missing Scarf

Kanga was very proud of her stripy knitted scarf. She had made it herself, and a smaller one for her son, Joey. Kanga used to hop along with her scarf streaming out behind her, while Joey's could just be seen poking out of the top of her pouch. Joey was too big for Kanga's pouch now, but he still wore his scarf as he hopped along.

Then one day Kanga lost her scarf. Although she searched high and low, it was nowhere to be found. Eventually she decided that she would have to go out into the bush to look for it.

Kanga hopped off and started to search among the roots of trees and under stones.

She had gone quite a long way when she spotted Koala. Koala was busy getting supper for her children. Kanga's jaw dropped – Koala was wearing Kanga's scarf around her tummy. Then, to Kanga's horror, she saw Koala use the end of the scarf to wipe the teacups! "Whatever do you think you're doing?" Kanga called.

Koala looked down through the branches of the eucalyptus tree at Kanga. "I'm wiping my teacups with my apron," she replied sleepily. And with that, she yawned and moved several branches further up the tree.

Poor Kanga, how could she have made such a mistake? She carried on further into the bush. She could hear Kookaburra's familiar laughing. "I know," thought Kanga, "she will be able to spot it from up in the sky." She followed the sound of Kookaburra's call until she came to her tree. She looked up and there was Kookaburra flying towards the tree. Her jaw dropped again. Kookaburra was carrying Kanga's scarf in her beak. "Whatever do you think you're doing?" Kanga called.

"I'm lining my nest," mumbled Kookaburra through a beakful of stripy feathers. "And I'll thank you not to interfere."

150

Poor Kanga, how could she have made
another mistake? She hopped away and carried
on further into the bush. After a while she saw
Emu running past with his baby chicks on his
back. Kanga's jaw dropped yet again. Emu had
Kanga's scarf tucked in among his chicks.
"What are you doing Emu?" she called.

"I'm taking my chicks to safety," said Emu,
"and you'd be wise to do the same." Then
Kanga realised her rolled-up scarf was really the
striped chicks on Emu's back.

Poor Kanga how could she have made yet
another mistake? She felt a few spots of rain on
her nose and saw a huge black cloud overhead.
She knew she must find shelter.

She made a dash for some trees and found herself by a stream. She wandered along until finally, she lay down in the wet grass beside the stream and tried to get to sleep. She shivered with cold and wondered how Joey was and whether he was behaving himself.

Just then Platypus tapped her on the shoulder. "I could hear you in my burrow over there," she said, "You might like this to keep you warm."

"My scarf!" exclaimed Kanga.

"I'm ever so sorry," said Platypus. "I've been using it as a blanket for my babies.

"Where did you find it?" asked Kanga.

"It was stuck on some thorns and I know I shouldn't have taken it, but I just thought it

would be so nice for keeping my young ones warm," and Platypus started to sob.

"There now," said Kanga, "don't cry. You can keep the scarf. You need it more than me."

Platypus smiled and thanked Kanga.

"No, thank you," said Kanga. "I've learned a lesson, which is not to get upset over a scarf. I've ended up falling out with my friends."

Kanga went home, and she apologised to all her friends on the way. When she explained what had happened Emu, Kookaburra and Koala all forgave her. "What have you been up to while I was away?" she asked Joey.

"I made you this," he said. He handed her a very funny-looking scarf, made out of twigs, grass and feathers. Kanga loved it very much.

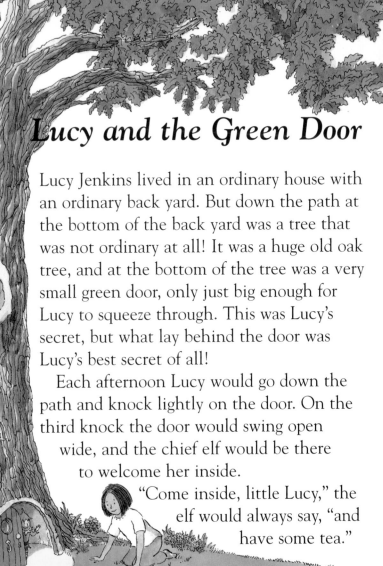

Lucy and the Green Door

Lucy Jenkins lived in an ordinary house with an ordinary back yard. But down the path at the bottom of the back yard was a tree that was not ordinary at all! It was a huge old oak tree, and at the bottom of the tree was a very small green door, only just big enough for Lucy to squeeze through. This was Lucy's secret, but what lay behind the door was Lucy's best secret of all!

Each afternoon Lucy would go down the path and knock lightly on the door. On the third knock the door would swing open wide, and the chief elf would be there to welcome her inside.

"Come inside, little Lucy," the elf would always say, "and have some tea."

154

Lucy would meet some
very special friends, two
of the gentlest and
sweetest fairies it was
possible to imagine,
Penelope and Geraldine.
Then there were Basil and
Granville, who were rather naughty
imps and the storytellers, who would sit with
Lucy telling her the greatest of tales. And
there was the chief elf, who would make the
most delicious milkshakes and scones with
heaps of cream for Lucy to eat.

Lucy would always go home afterwards feeling
very cheerful and jolly. On one visit Lucy had
just finished a scrumptious tea of cocoa and
toasted marshmallows with the chief elf, when
she went off to play games with Basil and
Granville. They were playing blind man's buff,
and Lucy roared with laughter as
Basil and Granville teased
each other.

Lucy had been feeling sad because soon she would go to school and only be able to visit her friends at weekends. They assured her that as long as she was always a true friend to them she could visit as often or as little as she liked. Then they took her to visit the storytellers who told her stories of how the whales learned to sing, and where the stars went when the sun rose in the sky and they slipped from view.

Because of the assurances of the fairies, Lucy was not too worried when the day finally came for her to start school. Every day, Lucy would go to school and then visit her friends behind the green door. As winter came round and the days grew dark she only visited at weekends, and looked forward to the holidays when she could visit them every day once more.

At school, Lucy had made friends with Jessica, and although she told Jessica all about her family and her home, she didn't tell her about her secret. Lucy did tell Jessica all the stories that she was told by the storytellers, and Jessica grew more and more curious about where she had heard all the wonderful tales. Jessica would ask more and more questions, and Lucy found it very difficult to avoid telling Jessica about her secret. Eventually, Lucy gave in and told her.

Jessica scoffed and laughed, she thought that Lucy was making the whole thing up! When Lucy protested, and said it was true, Jessica told her that it simply wasn't possible – that there were no such things as elves and fairies and imps and magical trees with green doors. Lucy was distraught, and decided to show Jessica.

On the way home Lucy started to worry. What if she really had imagined it all? Jessica walked beside Lucy, still teasing her and laughing about Lucy's 'invisible' friends!

Lucy was about to tap on the green door at the bottom of the oak tree when she noticed the door had disappeared – it simply wasn't there!

Jessica smirked and laughed, calling Lucy silly and babyish to believe in magic and fairy tales, and then ran off back down the road to school. When her mother saw her she thought Lucy must be ill – she looked so upset! Lucy went to bed early and cried herself to sleep.

While Lucy slept, she dreamt. All her elf friends were there in the dream. Then Penelope and Geraldine stepped forward and hugged Lucy, and the hug was so real that Lucy hoped it wasn't a dream! Then they all hugged her and asked why she hadn't been to see them for so long. Lucy explained what had happened. "Little Lucy," Geraldine said, "you believe in magic and little people. Because you believe, you are able to see us and live among us. But those who don't believe will always be shut out from our world. You must keep your belief, little Lucy because you are special."

Lucy woke up and ran into the yard to the extraordinary tree, and and there was the green door! After the third tap, the door swung open to reveal the chief elf. "Come inside, little Lucy and have some tea," he said happily.

Ursula's Umbrella

Ursula longed for adventure. "Why doesn't anything interesting ever happen to me?" she sighed. "I wish I could fly to the moon or dive to the the deepest part of the ocean!"

One day Ursula went out for a walk. As it looked as though it might rain she took her umbrella. Ursula's umbrella was red with a shiny black handle and was very large indeed. It looked so big and Ursula was so small that it seemed as though the umbrella was walking along all by itself!

URSULA'S UMBRELLA

Ursula felt raindrops so she unfurled her umbrella and lifted it up above her head. A great gust of wind swept her right off the pavement, carried her past the upstairs windows of the houses, past the roofs and the chimney pots and up, up, into the sky. Ursula clung tightly to the umbrella handle. She felt very excited. Looking down she saw streets, factories, fields and a river snaking through the countryside.

Soon the umbrella was carrying her out over the ocean. At first the sea was gray, but slowly it turned to the deepest blue with frothy white waves. At that moment the umbrella started to descend. She could see they were heading for an island. She began to float past the tops of palm trees and, as she touched the ground, she felt sand under her feet.

URSULA'S UMBRELLA

"I'm going for a swim!" decided Ursula, and folding up her umbrella, she set off to the beach. The water was deliciously warm. As she looked down she could see that the water was amazingly clear. Brightly colored fish darted in and out of the coral. But as Ursula looked up she saw a black fin skimming through the water towards her. "Shark!" she shrieked, but no-one heard.

Suddenly a gust of wind unfurled her umbrella and it floated to her, like a boat. Ursula hurled herself into it and floated away. "That was quite an adventure!" she thought.

URSULA'S UMBRELLA

After a while Ursula saw she was heading for the shore. When Ursula stepped out of the umbrella, she found that she was at the edge of a jungle. Folding up the umbrella, she set off. She wiped her brow and swatted the insects that flew in front of her face. She went deeper and deeper into the jungle.

Suddenly she heard the sound of rushing water and found herself standing on the banks of a river. Then she heard the crashing noise of an enormous beast coming through the trees.

She felt the umbrella being blown from her hand. It fell to the ground, stretching right across the river like a bridge and Ursula walked over to the other side. Safely on the far bank, she looked back to see a large puma glaring at her. "That was a lucky escape!" thought Ursula.

Ursula decided to head towards a mountain. "The view from the top may help me find my way home," she thought. But when she reached it there was no way up the sheer rock face.

Ursula was on the point of despair when another great gust of wind blew up. It carried Ursula all the way up to the top of the mountain.

164

URSULA'S UMBRELLA

At the top of the mountain, she landed in deep snow with a blizzard blowing. "There's only one thing to do," thought Ursula. She put the umbrella on the snow, sat in it and whizzed all the way down the mountain.

When she reached the bottom the umbrella sledge didn't stop. Eventually, it came to a halt right outside her own front door. "Well, that was quite an adventure," said Ursula.

"Wherever have you been?" said her mother. "You look as though you've been to the ends of the Earth and back."

"Well I have," Ursula was about to say. But then she thought that no-one would believe her and it was nicer to keep her adventures to herself. And that is what she did.

The Sleeping Beauty

In a land far away, there ruled the happiest
king and queen who had ever lived. They
were especially happy because they had finally
borne a beautiful baby daughter.

They decided to throw a huge banquet for
their family, friends, and all the important
people in the kingdom. They were writing
the invitations when the queen said to her
husband, "The Countess Griselda will be very
angry if we don't invite her."

The king shook his head and said, "No, she must not be invited. Griselda is wicked and mean. I do not wish her to cast her eyes on our beautiful daughter."

The day of the banquet arrived, and all the most important people took their places in the Great Hall. Before the celebrations began, twelve people stood in line to give their gifts to the princess, who was sleeping in her cradle next to the royal thrones.

First was Lady Soprano, who declared the princess would have a voice like an angel. Next came the Archduke Ernest who vowed she would grow to be very wise. Next came the Duchess Rose, declaring she would blossom into the most beautiful flower in the kingdom.

One by one the guests gave gifts of patience, kindness, faith, grace, fortune, happiness, virtue, and sweetness. Suddenly there was a terrible noise outside the Great Hall and in stormed the Countess Griselda. Everyone fell silent. As she approached the sleeping baby, Griselda swept aside the king and queen.

Griselda turned to them and whispered in a hard, cruel voice, "I think you mislaid my invitation." She bent over the child, cackling, "To this child I bestow the gift of absolute health until the day she dies." Then she turned to the crowd, "Which is why it is such a pity she will not live beyond her sixteenth birthday!"

She continued, "A spindle shall be her end. A common peasant's spindle," touching the tip of the middle finger on the baby's right hand. Then Griselda disappeared, leaving only her terrible spell behind her.

Marquess Maria, the final guest bent over Angelina whispering, "I cannot take away the evil of Griselda, but I can give you the gift of love. On that terrible day you shall not die a death, but sleep, until love comes to rescue you." She placed her forefinger on the baby's heart and then was gone.

In despair the king and queen demanded the destruction of every spindle in the land. But they couldn't sleep at night without worrying, and they never let the little princess out of their sight for a moment.

Angelina grew, and with every passing year she became sweeter, and with every passing day she became more beautiful.

Angelina's birthday arrived, and for the first time ever the king and queen allowed her to roam freely around the castle. There was to be a huge celebration, and Angelina had great fun watching the cooks prepare delicious pies, pastries, and cakes, and roamed through all the corridors to watch the preparations.

In a corridor off the Great Hall, she found a trail of petals, winding this way and that, up into a turret in the castle that she had never visited before. At the top, a door swung open and in the corner of the darkened room a little old lady sat spinning some yarn.

"Come closer, my child," she beckoned.

Angelina moved closer.

"Closer still," she urged.

When Angelina was close enough the old woman reached out to Angelina's right hand and pulled it to the needle. It pricked her middle finger, and she fell into a deep and most peaceful sleep. The whole castle fell asleep – the cooks, the horses, even the king. Everything in the castle came to a complete and utter standstill.

The legend of the sleeping beauty spread to distant lands. Many brave princes tried to cut down the thorns that had grown around the castle, but without success.

After years had passed a brave prince awoke from a dream in which the angelic voice of a girl had called to him from a thorn bush. He asked his father the meaning of the dream, but the king shook his head and refused to tell him.

But the following night, the young prince again dreamed of the girl. This time he saw the princess deep in sleep, calling to be freed. Again he asked his father who she was and again the king refused to tell him, but the prince's dreams continued and eventually the king relented.

The prince lost no time in trying to find the princess. He set off on a voyage that lasted a year and a day. Along the way he heard tales of the princes who had tried before and their strange fates, but none had succeeded.

Finally the prince reached his destination outside the walls of the thorn forest. He raised his sword to strike the thorns. In that instant, a vision of the princess rose up to him, and he was so overcome with love that he dropped his sword and tried to touch the vision. In reaching out he touched the thorns, and they turned into flowers. The forest bowed down before him, until all that separated him from the princess was a carpet of roses. Racing past the sleeping horses, cooks, and the king, the prince ran to where the princess lay. He bent over her and placed a single kiss on her lips. She opened her eyes – love had set her free.

Everyone in the castle woke up. The king was overjoyed and granted the prince any wish that he could choose. The prince asked for the princess's hand in marriage, and they both lived happily ever after.

Rusty's Big Day

Long ago a poor farmer called Fred had a horse called Rusty. Once Rusty had been a fine, strong horse, willing to pull the plough and take his master into town to sell his vegetables. Now he was too old to work, but the farmer couldn't bear to lose him because he was so gentle. Rusty spent his days grazing. He was content, but sad that he could no longer help the poor farmer.

One day Fred harnessed Beauty, the young mare, to the wagon and they went to market to sell some vegetables. Beauty glanced at Rusty as if to say, "Look who's queen of the farmyard!"

RUSTY'S BIG DAY

While Fred was in the town, he saw
a notice pinned to a tree. It said:

Horse Parade at 2 pm today
The winner will pull the king's carriage
to the Grand Banquet tonight

"There's not a moment to lose, my girl!" said
Fred. "We must get you ready for the parade,"
and they trotted all the way back to the farm.
Fred set to work to make Beauty look even
more lovely. He scrubbed her hoofs, brushed
her coat, plaited her mane and tied it with a
bright red ribbon. "How fine she looks," Rusty
thought, wistfully. "She's sure to win."
He felt a bit sad that he was too old to
take part in the parade.

All at once, he heard Fred approach. "Come on, old boy," he said, "it'll be fun for you to watch the parade, won't it?" Rusty was thrilled.

Soon the three of them set off back into town, with Fred riding on Beauty's back and Rusty walking by their side. When they reached the parade ground, there were horses of every shape and size – small, skinny ones, big, muscular ones, and there were even big, skinny ones, too!

The king and memebers of the court entered the parade ground. Then the king announced three contests. First there would be a race. The horses would gallop from one end of the parade ground to the other. Then there would be a

contest of strength. Each horse would
pull a heavy carriage. Lastly, there would be
a trotting competition. Each horse would have
to carry a rider around the parade ground.

All the horses lined up at the starting line.
"Come on, Rusty. Have a go!" whispered Fred.
He led Rusty and Beauty to where the other
horses were lined up.

All the other horses turned and stared,
whispering that Rusty was too old. Rusty said
nothing and took his place at the start. Then
they were off down the field. Rusty felt his feet
fly, but he couldn't keep up and came in last.

"What did you expect?" snorted the other
horses. However, Rusty was not downcast.
"Speed isn't everything," he said to himself.

Now it was the test of strength. The horses took it in turns to pull the carriage. Rusty tried his best he felt every muscle in his aching body strain but as he slowly pulled the carriage along.

"Not a hope!" declared the other horses.

"Strength isn't everything," said Rusty.

Next was the trotting competition. The king rode each horse in turn. The first horse bolted, leaving the king hanging by the stirrups. The next threw the king up in the air and was caught by one of his courtiers. The next horse was so nervous that his teeth chattered, and the king had to put his fingers in his ears. Beauty carried the king magnificently, until she stumbled at the end. When it was Rusty's turn the other horses sniggered at him.

Rusty carried the king slowly and steadily, so that his royal highness would not be jolted. "Thank you for a most pleasant ride," said the king. Everyone awaited the result of the contest. "I have decided," announced the king, "that Rusty is the winner. He give me a comfortable ride, and he accepted his other defeats with dignity. Speed and strength are not everything."

Rusty and Fred were overjoyed, and even Beauty offered her congratulations. So Rusty proudly pulled the king's carriage that evening. Then the king asked him if he would do it the next year, and he asked Fred if his daughter could ride Beauty. He gave Fred a bag of gold to pay for the horses' upkeep, so the three of them were happier than they had ever been before.

179

The Very Big Parcel

Once upon a time an old man and his wife lived in a small house with a small, neat vegetable patch and they were very contented. They had very good friends and neighbors, with whom they shared everything. One day, the postman came to the door with a huge parcel in his arms.

"My, oh my!" exclaimed the old man to his wife as he stared at the enormous load.

"Perhaps it's a new set of china," said she.

"Or a new wheelbarrow," said he. And they began to think about the fancy things that might be the parcel.

"Why don't we open it and see?" said the old lady. They looked into the box and at first it seemed to be totally empty. Then the old man spotted something in the corner of the box. He lifted it out and discovered it was a single seed!

Now that they had thought about all the things that might have been in the box they were bitterly disappointed by the seed. "Still," said the old man, "we'd better plant it anyway. Who knows what it might turn into."

Every day he watered the ground and soon a shoot appeared. The shoot grew taller and higher until it was a handsome tree. The man and his wife were excited to see fruits growing on the tree. Each day he watered the tree and examined the fruits. One day he said to his wife, "The first fruit is ready to pick." He carefully reached up into the tree

He carried it into the kitchen and cut it in half. To his astonishment out poured a pile of gold coins. The old man and his wife danced round the kitchen for joy.

The old couple decided to spend just one gold coin and keep the rest. "After all," said the woman wisely, "the other fruits may be full of worms." So they spent one golden penny in the town and put the rest aside.

The next fruit was full of gold too. After that they were less careful with their money, thinking all the fruits must be full of gold.

Each day the man picked another fruit. Each day it was full of gold and each day they went into town and had a grand time spending the money. But all the while the man forgot entirely to water the tree.

Meanwhile, their friends and neighbors wondered where all the money was coming from and they noticed that the old couple didn't buy anything for their friends, or even throw a party. The old couple were left with no friends at all. But they didn't notice because they were busy spending the gold coins.

One day the old man saw that the tree was withered. He rushed outside and threw bucket after bucket of water over the tree.

He and his wife picked the fruits, but when they took them indoors they found that they were cracked and full of dust. "If only I had not been so thoughtless and remembered to water the tree!" cried the old man in anguish.

The next day the tree had vanished. Now what were they to do? They had completely neglected to take care of their vegetable patch and now they had nothing to eat.

As the weeks passed, the old man and his wife gradually sold all the fine things they had bought, just to keep body and soul together. They felt truly miserable and sorry for the way

they had treated their neighbors.
Now they realized just how lonely
they were without their friends.
"We have no money now," said the
wife one day, "but let's have a party
anyway. Friendship is more valuable
than any amount of gold coins."

So the old couple invited all their
friends and neighbors round and
they had a grand party. The friends
wondered what had happened to all
the old couple's riches and what had
happened to make the old couple
so friendly once more, but I don't
think they ever found out, do you?

Little Tim and His Brother Sam

Little Tim was a very lucky boy. He had the nicest parents you could hope for, and a back yard, with a swing and a basketball net. Little Tim even had a nice school where he had lots of friends. In fact, everything in Tim's life was nice apart from one thing – his brother Sam.

Sam was a very naughty boy and whenever he got into mischief he managed to make it look as though someone else was to blame. And that someone was usually Tim!

Once Sam put salt in the sugar bowl instead of sugar. Sam and Tim's parents had friends round for tea and all the guests put salt in their cups of tea, thinking it was sugar. When Sam and Tim's parents tasted their tea they guessed immediately that someone had been playing a trick and they had to apologize to their guests. Who got the blame? Little Tim, because Sam had sprinkled salt on Tim's bedroom floor so that it looked as if Tim was guilty.

Another time, out in the yard, Sam kicked the ball against a window and broke it. Sam immediately ran away and hid, so that only Tim was to be seen. So poor little Tim got the blame again.

Then Sam and Tim's Aunt Jessica came to stay.
She hated frogs. So what did Sam do? He went
down to the pond in the back yard and got a
big, green frog to put in Aunt Jessica's handbag.
When Aunt Jessica opened her handbag, there
staring at her were two froggy eyes.

"Croak!" said the frog.

"Eeek!" yelled Aunt Jessica and almost jumped
out of her skin.

"I told Tim not to do it," said Sam.

"Tim, go to your room and don't come out
until you are told,"
said his mother.

188

Poor Tim had to stay there until after supper. Sam thought it was very funny.

The next day, Sam decided that he would play another prank and blame it on Tim. He went to the tool shed and took out all the tools and hid them all in Tim's bedroom.

But this time, Sam's little prank was about to come unstuck. Aunt Jessica had seen him creeping up the stairs to Tim's bedroom. She guessed immediately what Sam was up to. When Sam wasn't about, she spoke to Tim. The two of them whispered to each other for a few seconds and then smiled triumphantly.

Later that day, the boys' father went to the tool shed. Imagine his surprise when all he saw were some flower pots and the lawnmower. He searched high and low for the tools, but they weren't anywhere to be seen.

He had started searching in the house. when something at the top of the stairs caught his eye. The handle from the spade was sticking out of the door to Sam's bedroom. Looking rather puzzled, he went upstairs and walked into Sam's bedroom. There in the cupboard, were all the tools.

"Sam, come up here now," called his father.

As Sam came up stairs he saw all the tools sitting in *his* cupboard. He was speechless.

"Right," said his father, "you can take all the tools back down to the shed. Then you can cut the grass, dig over the flower beds, and then you can do the weeding."

That took Sam hours. Tim and Aunt Jessica watched from the window, clutching their sides with laughter. Sam didn't find out how all the garden tools found their way into his bedroom, but I think you've guessed, haven't you?

Peter Meets a Dragon

A young boy named Peter lived in an ordinary
house with an ordinary Mom and Dad, an
ordinary sister and an ordinary pet cat, called
Jasper. "Why is everything so ordinary? Why
doesn't a giant come and squash the house flat
with his foot?" he wondered, and "If only a
pirate would take my sister hostage!"

One morning Peter woke up to find a strange
smell in the house. Looking out of his bedroom
window, he saw the front lawn was scorched and
blackened. Smoke was drifting off the grass and,
further away, he could see some bushes ablaze.

PETER MEETS A DRAGON

Peter rushed downstairs to follow the trail of smoke and burning grass. After a while he heard a panting noise coming from the bushes. He looked around and found a young creature with green, scaly skin, a pair of wings and a long snout full of sharp teeth. A little tongue of flame came from its nostrils, setting the grass around it on fire – a baby dragon! Big tears were rolling out of the dragon's yellow eyes and down its scaly cheeks as it flapped its wings desperately and tried to take off.

The dragon saw Peter. "Oh, woe is me!" it sobbed. "Where am I?"

"Where do you want to be?" asked Peter, as he knelt down.

"I want to be with my friends," replied the dragon. "We were all flying, but I couldn't keep up with them. I needed a rest so I called to the others but they didn't hear me. I just had to stop and get my breath back. Now I don't know where I am, or if I'll ever see my friends again!" And the baby dragon started to cry once more.

"I'm sure I can help. " said Peter.

"You?" hissed a voice nearby. "How could you possibly help? You're just a boy!" Peter looked round and found Jasper behind him. "I suppose you're going to wave a magic wand, are you?" continued Jasper. Then he turned his back on them both and washed his paws.

Peter was astounded. He had thought Jasper was just an ordinary pet cat. "W… w…what do you mean?" he stammered.

"Well," said Jasper, "The horse over there could help. Follow me." So they both followed Jasper over to the edge of a field. Jasper leaned over the gate and whispered in the horse's ear. The horse whispered back. "He says he's got a friend who can help," said Jasper.

"But how?" said Peter, looking perplexed.

"Follow me!" said Jasper, "and tell your friend to stop setting fire to everything!" he added. Peter saw, to his horror, that Flame, the young dragon, was blazing a trail through the field.

"I can't help it," cried Flame. "Every time I get out of breath I start to pant, and then I start breathing fire."

"Let me carry you," said Peter, picking up Flame and running. His body was all cold and clammy, but his mouth was still breathing hot smoke, which made Peter's eyes water.

On the other side of the wood was a field, with another horse, but this was no ordinary horse. Peter stopped and stared. The horse was pure milky white, and from its head grew a single, long horn. "A unicorn!" breathed Peter.

Jasper beckoned with his paw to Peter. "He'll take your friend home and you can go Peter, but don't be late for tea." Then Jasper was off.

"Climb aboard," said the unicorn gently.

Peter and the little dragon scrambled up on to the unicorn's back. They soared through the clouds until at last Peter could see a mountain through the clouds. Then they descended and the unicorn landed right at the top of the mountain. "I'm home!" squeaked Flame joyously as they landed. Sure enough, several dragons came over to greet him. They looked friendly, but some of them were rather large and one was breathing a great deal of fire.

"Time for me to go," said Peter a little nervously. The unicorn took off again and soon they were back in the field once more.

Peter turned to thank the unicorn, but he was just an ordinary horse with no trace of a horn at all. Peter walked back home, but there was no sign of burnt grass. "Jasper will explain," he thought. But when he asked Jasper, the cat said nothing. He ignored Peter and closed his eyes.

When Peter wasn't looking, however, Jasper gave him a glance that seemed to say, "Well, was that a big enough adventure for you?"

The Greedy Hamster

Harry was a very greedy hamster. As soon as he was given food he gobbled it up, and then he would push his little nose through the bars to find something else to eat. From his cage he could see delicious food on the kitchen table and the scent of freshly baked bread was enough to send him spinning round in his exercise wheel with frustration.

"It's not fair!" he grumbled to himself. "They are all eating and I am simply starving to death!" (At this point he would usually remember that he had just eaten a large meal and and that his tummy was indeed still rather full.)

"If only I could get out of this cage, I could have all the food I deserve," he said to himself.

One night after the family had gone to bed, Harry was having one last spin in his wheel before retiring to his sawdust mattress. As he spun around, he heard an unfamiliar squeaky noise.

He stopped running but the squeak continued. Harry sat quite still on his haunches and listened intently. Then he realized it was the door to his cage squeaking! The little girl had not closed it properly before she went to bed. Harry looked cautiously out in case there was any danger. The cat was asleep on a chair. The dog was sleeping soundly on the floor – all seemed to be quite safe.

Harry was clever as well as greedy. He looked at the catch to see how it worked, and yes, was sure he could open it from the inside now.

Harry sniffed the air. There were some tasty titbits on the table. Soon he was on the table, cramming his mouth with odds and ends of cheese sandwiches and pieces of chocolate cake. Then he stuffed his cheek pouches with ginger biscuits and ran back into his cage, closing the door behind him, thinking, "Good, now I will never be hungry again."

Harry let himself out of his cage and helped himself to food the next night and the night after that. He feasted on everything and anything – nuts, bananas, pieces of bread and slices of pizza. When he returned to his cage he filled his cheeks with more food. Although he couldn't run round in his wheel without falling off, he didn't notice he was getting fatter until one night, he couldn't get through the door!

For a while Harry sat in a very bad temper in the corner of the cage. Although his cheeks bulged with food from his last night, the greedy hamster wanted more. Then he thought "I'll get that lazy cat to help." He squealed until the cat, who had been dreaming of rats, woke up.

"What do you want?" she hissed at Harry. Harry explained his problem.

"Of course I will help," said the crafty cat! With her strong claws she bent the door frame until Harry could just squeeze through. Then, with a swipe of her paw, she caught him and gobbled him whole. She felt extremely full and soon she was fast asleep on her chair, snoring loudly with her mouth open. Inside the cat's tummy it sounded like a thunderstorm raging around Harry's head every time she snored.

"I must get out of here," he thought, heading for the cat's open jaws. But again, he was too fat to get out. Then he had another idea. He could see the dog lying on the floor.

"Help! Help!" he squeaked. The dog woke up to a very strange sight – the cat was lying on the chair snoring *and* squeaking, "Help!" The dog was very perplexed. Then he saw Harry!

THE GREEDY HAMSTER

"Get me out of here, please," pleaded Harry.

Now the dog did not like the cat, so he was quite willing to help the hamster.

"I'll stick my tail in the cat's mouth. Then you hang on while I pull you out," said the dog. "But don't make a sound and wake the cat, or she'll bite my tail!" The dog gingerly put the tip of his tail inside the cat's open jaws, just far enough for Harry's little paws to grab hold. Then he pulled with all his might and out popped Harry

"Thank you, thank you," gasped Harry as he made a dash for his cage and slammed the door shut. "I think I'll stay in my cage from now on and just eat the food that I am given!"

The Invisible Imp

One lovely day, Sarah Jones was pegging out her washing. She was looking forward to visiting her friend Rose, "I'll just get this washing on the line while the sun's shining," she said to herself, "and then I'll leave."

"That's peculiar!" she thought after a while. "I've already pegged out that green shirt and there it is back in the basket." She carried on pegging out the clothes, then she shook her head in disbelief. The basket of washing was still full and there was almost nothing on the line! She began to get quite cross, she was going to be late.

She just could not get the washing on the line and in the end, she had to leave the basket of wet washing and run to Rose's house.

"I'm so sorry I'm late, Rose," she gasped, and explained what had happened.

"Well," said Rose, "that's a coincidence. I was baking some cakes for us to have for tea. Every time I put them in the oven they were out of the oven and on the table again! In the end I had to stand guard over them – which reminds me, they were just beginning to cook nicely when you knocked on the door."

They went into Rose's kitchen to find the cakes on the table again, half-cooked. "Now they're ruined!" cried Rose. "Whatever shall we do?"

Suddenly, Elmer the mailman, was surrounded by a crowd of people all shouting and waving envelopes in the air. The two women ran into the street. "What's going on?" they cried.

"Elmer's given us all the wrong mail," said Rose's neighbor, "and now we've got to sort out all the mail for him."

"I don't know what's happened," wailed Elmer in anguish. "I'm sure I sorted the mail."

"Well," said Sarah, "Rose and I have had strange things happening to us this morning." She told the crowd their stories. Everyone forgave Elmer when they realized it wasn't his fault, but they were still mystified about the cause of all these problems.

But that wasn't the end of it. The butcher's wife served her family mutton stew, but when she lifted the lid a little lamb leaped out of the pot. The milkman delivered the milk, but people found the bottles full of lemonade. Mrs Smith painted her bedroom blue, she came back and found it had changed to pink with purple spots.

Can you guess what had happened? It was an imp, of course! The wicked little fellow had become bored playing pranks in fairyland. Then he had an idea. Why not play tricks in the human world where he would be invisible? So that's exactly what he did.

He really only meant to play one or two tricks, but he had such fun that he couldn't resist carrying on. But one day, of course, he just went too far. Sarah Jones had been invited to a fancy dress party and on the invitation it said: "*Please wear red*". Sarah fretted because she had no red clothes at all. Then she had an idea, she got out an old blue frock. "I'll dye it red," she thought.

Just as Sarah was about to put the dress into a big bowl of dye, along came the invisible imp. "Here's some fun!" he thought. "I'll turn the dye blue. Won't that be funny!" And he started giggling to himself at the very thought of it. He danced up and down on the edge of the tub, thinking up a really evil spell but he laughed so much to himself that he slipped and fell right into the bright red mixture. He scrambled out and cast his spell.

When Sarah fished out the dress from the tub she saw to her dismay that it was exactly the same colour. She was about to peer into the tub when something caught her eye. Sitting on the table, chuckling to himself and holding his sides with laughter, was a bright red imp. The silly imp had no idea that he was no longer invisible and that Sarah could see him! In a flash Sarah realised what had happened. She chased the imp out of the house and down the street. Thanks to Sarah, he wasn't able to play his mischievous tricks ever again.

The Three Little Pigs

Once upon a time three little pigs lived with their parents. Although they were little pigs, they were quite grown up, so one day they set off together to make their fortunes in the world.

They had walked for quite some time when one of the little pigs started to feel tired. Just then, a farmer went by on his haycart. The first little pig stopped the cart, saying to his brothers. "You stronger brothers go on. This hay is light and soft enough for my house." And so his brothers left the little pig and carried on their journey.

A little further down the road, the second little pig grew very tired. Just then, they passed by a forester cutting wood. "This wood is just right for my house, would you sell me some?" asked the second little pig And so the third little pig carried on with his journey. The third little pig grew was soon very tired when he spotted a builder making a wall out of stone.

"Aha," he thought, "that's strong and tough, just like me." And so he bought some stone and built himself a house.

The first little pig was settling comfortably in his bed of hay that night when he heard a noise outside the house. He looked through the hay walls and gulped in fright when he saw the big bad wolf looking at him greedily.

"Little piggy, little piggy, will you let me in?"

"Not by the hairs of my chinny chin chin, I will not let you in," shuddered the first little pig.

"Then I'll huff, and I'll puff, and I'll blow your house down," said the big bad wolf.

Sure enough, he gave a little huff and a little puff, and he blew the house down. The little pig ran away as fast as his little legs would carry him to the home of his nearest brother.

The next evening, the two brothers were
eating their dinner when they heard scratching
outside the house. They gasped when they saw
the big bad wolf staring at them hungrily.

"Little piggies, little piggies, will you
let me in?"

"Not by the hairs of our chinny
chin chins, we will not let you in,"
trembled the little pigs.

"Then I'll huff, and I'll puff,
and I'll blow your house down,"
said the big
bad wolf.

And sure enough, he huffed and he puffed, and with some effort he blew the house down. The two pigs ran away as fast as their little legs would carry them to the home of their brother.

The next evening, the three brothers lit a fire to warm their toes. They heard crashing outside the house so the third little pig pulled a stone out of the wall, and they all shrieked in terror when they saw the big bad wolf staring at them. His stomach rumbled, and he was smacking his lips at the feast waiting just a short breath away!

"Little piggies, little piggies, will you let me in?"

"Not by the hairs of our chinny chin chins, we will not let you in," said the three little pigs.

"Then I'll huff, and I'll puff, and I'll blow your house down," said the big bad wolf.

And sure enough, he took a huff, and he took a puff, and he blew. But the house didn't blow down. So he took a bigger huff and a bigger puff, and he blew. But the house still didn't blow down. So with a mighty effort he blew and blew and blew! And the house stayed up!

Then the big bad wolf started to climb up the stone wall to the chimney. The three little pigs looked around the room but there was nowhere to hide, and nowhere to run. They would have to stand and fight the big bad wolf!

One of the little pigs had an idea, and told his brothers. They hooked a huge pot of water over the roaring fire. They heard the wolf climb into the chimney as the water in the pot started to steam. The wolf climbing down the chimney as the water started to bubble. The wolf slid down the chimney and he landed splash in the middle of the pot of now boiling water. PLOP!

The big bad wolf screamed and leaped out of the boiling pot. The three little pigs ran around to get away from the wolf, as the big bad wolf ran around trying to cool down. Eventually he burst through the wall, and ran screaming and shouting through the woods. That was the last they ever saw of him.

The three little pigs knew they were safe now, so they decided to build a new, cozy house. The walls were of tough, strong stone. The tables were of smooth, warm wood, and they used soft, fresh hay to make comfortable beds. It was the best house in the world, and they all lived in it happily ever after.

The Lost Lion

Once there was a very tiny lion cub called
Lenny. He was sure that he was the bravest lion
in all of Africa. When his mother taught her
cubs how to stalk prey, Lenny would stalk her
and pounce on her. When his mother showed
them how to wash, Lenny licked his sister's face
instead so that she growled at him. When his
mother led her cubs down to the watering hole
to drink, he jumped into the water and created
a huge splash that soaked everyone.

The other lionesses complained. "You'd better
watch that son of yours," they said to Lenny's
mother, "or he'll get into really big trouble."

One day the mother lioness led her cubs on their first hunt. "Stay close," she said, "or you could get hurt."

She crawled off through the undergrowth with her cubs following on behind. Lenny was at the back. He crawled along, making sure he kept the bobbing tail of the cub in front in sight. On and on they crawled until Lenny was beginning to feel quite weary.

"But a brave lion cub doesn't give up," he thought to himself. And on he plodded.

At last the grass gave way to a clearing. Lenny looked up, and to his dismay he saw that the tail he had been following was attached, not to one of his brothers or sisters, but to a baby elephant!

He had followed the wrong tail and was lost. He wanted to shout for his mother but then he remembered that he was the bravest lion in Africa. So what did he do? He went up to the mother elephant and growled fiercely at her. "She won't dare growl back!" thought Lenny. Instead of growling, she trumpeted so loudly that Lenny was blown off his feet, through the air and landed against the hard trunk of a tree.

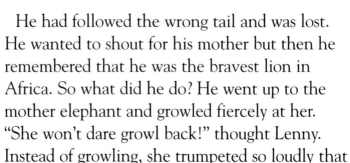

"Oh my," he thought, "that elephant has a very loud growl. But I'm still definitely the bravest lion in all of Africa." He set off across the plain, but Lenny began to feel sleepy in the midday sun. "I think I'll just take a nap in that tree," he thought, and climbed the branches.

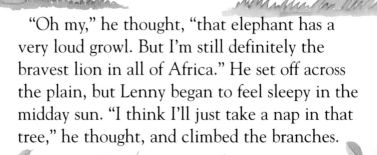

To his surprise, he found the tree was already occupied by a leopard. "I'll show him who's boss," thought Lenny, baring his tiny claws. The leopard looked at Lenny, and took a swipe at Lenny with his own huge, razor-sharp claws. The wind from the leopard's great paw swept Lenny out of the tree and he landed with a bump on the ground.

Lenny got up and found that his legs were trembling. "Oh my," he thought, "that leopard had big claws. But I'm still definitely the bravest lion in Africa." He set off again across the plain. After a while he began to feel quite hungry. "I wonder what I can find to eat," he thought. Just then he saw a spotted shape lying low in the grass. "That looks like a tasty meal," thought Lenny, and he pounced on the spotted shape.

But the spotted shape was a cheetah! The cheetah sprang away and his tail caught Lenny a blow that sent him spinning round in circles.

Lenny found that his whole body was shaking. "Oh my," he thought, that cheetah is a fast runner." Then he added in rather a small voice, "But I'm still the bravest lion in Africa." It was getting dark as he set off again across the plain and Lenny was wishing he was at home. He felt cold and tired and hungry as he crawled into the undergrowth to sleep.

Lenny was woken by a noise that was louder than anything he'd ever heard before – louder even than the elephant's trumpeting. It filled the night air and the leaves on the trees shook. The noise was getting louder and louder and

nearer and nearer. Lenny peeped out and saw a huge golden creature with a crown of shaggy golden fur all around its head. Its red jaws were open wide revealing a set of very large white fangs. How it roared! Suddenly the animal stopped roaring and spoke to him. "Come here, Lenny," said the animal gently. "It's me, your father, and I'm here to take you home. Climb up on my back, little one."

So Lenny climbed up on his father's back and was carried all the way home. And when they got there his father told all his family that Lenny had been a very brave lion after all.

Buried Treasure

Jim lived in a old house with a big rambling back yard. Jim loved playing out there, he would spend hours kicking a football on the overgrown lawn, climbing the old apple trees or trying to spot a fish in the pond. But Jim was not really a happy child because he was lonely. It would be such fun to play football with a friend, or have someone to go fishing with. It was a long bus journey for his school friends and they found his house so spooky that they only came to visit once.

BURIED TREASURE

One day Jim was hunting about for some small creatures to examine. So far, he had discovered eight types of snails and six different ladybugs. As he was poking under some leaves he saw a piece of metal sticking out of the ground. He pulled free a big, rusty old key that was carved with beautiful patterns.

After Jim had cleaned and polished the key he set about finding the lock that it fitted. He tried the old gate that had been locked for as long as Jim could remember, but the key was far too small. Next he tried the grandfather clock in the hall, but the key did not fit. Then he remembered an old wind-up teddy bear, but this time it was too big.

Then Jim remembered the attic. He was usually too scared to go into the attic on his own, but now he was so determined to find the key's home that he ran up the stairs boldly and opened the door. The attic was dimly lit, dusty and full of cobwebs. The water pipes hissed and creaked and Jim shivered. At first he didn't find anything that looked like it needed a key to unlock it. Then he caught sight of a large book with a lock sticking out from one of the shelves. His fingers trembled as he put the key in the lock. It fitted perfectly and the lock sprang open, releasing a cloud of dust. Jim opened the book and turned the pages.

What a disappointment! There were no pictures and each page was covered with tiny writing. Then Jim heard a voice coming from the book! "You have unlocked my secrets," it said. "Step into my pages if you are looking for adventure."

Jim put his foot on the pages and found he was falling through the book and onto the deck of a ship. Flying high above was a skull and cross-bones flag. He was on a pirate ship and he was dressed like a pirate!

Looking up Jim saw they were heading straight for some very dangerous looking rocks! Before he could shout, the ship ran aground and all the pirates jumped overboard and swam to the shore. Jim swam, too.

The water felt deliciously warm and he swam ashore to a desert island. The pirates went in all directions, searching for somewhere to take shelter. Jim looked, too, and under a rock he found a book that looked familiar. He was puzzling over it when one of the pirates ran towards him waving a knife. "You thief, you stole me rubies!" What was Jim to do?

A voice called out from the book, "Step into my pages, quickly." Jim stepped straight into the book and he was back in the attic again.

Jim peered at the open book. He read *The Pirates and the Stolen Treasure* at the top of the page, and it was the adventure he had been in. He turned excitedly to the contents page and read the titles. *Journey to Mars, The Castle Under the Sea, The Magic Car* and *Into the Jungle.* Jim realized that he could become part of any adventure, and he only had to step into the book to get back to the attic again.

Jim had many, many adventures. He made lots of friends in the stories and he had lots of narrow escapes. But he always found the book again just in time. Jim was never lonely again.

Catswhiskers

Catswhiskers was a very fine looking pajamas case cat. Susie's granny had sewn him when Susie was four years old. Every night she had sat by the fire carefully cutting and sewing, until he was perfect. Catswhiskers' body was made from the finest black velvet. He had beautiful red glass eyes, a bushy tail and the longest whiskers you have ever seen, which is how he got his name. Catswhiskers sat on the end of Susie's bed, looking at all the toys in that slightly snooty way that cats have of looking at things.

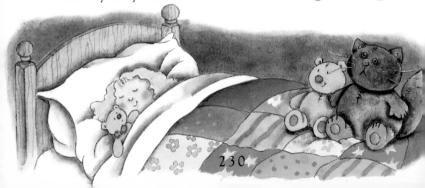

CATSWHISKERS

When Susie wasn't in the room, all the toys would talk to each other. But this bored Catswhiskers. Jenny the rag doll was – well – just a ragdoll. "What could a rag doll possibly have to say that would be of interest to a velvet pyjama case cat?" thought Catswhiskers.

Then there was Neddy the rocking horse, a perfectly pleasant rocking horse, but he only ever seemed to want to talk about how nice and shiny he was, and how he thought he was Susie's favorite toy. None of the toys seemed to have anything of interest to say to Catswhiskers. He sighed and looked at the window, wondering if life was more exciting outside.

One day, he decided he'd had enough of life
in the bedroom, and that he would venture
outside to see if he could meet someone more
interesting. So that night, he crept carefully to
the open bedroom window and jumped out into
the clear, moonlit night. Catswhiskers shivered
a little to find it so cold outside. But he was
very excited to be in the outside world, too, and
he soon forgot about the cold and his fear.

He walked along the fence and jumped down
into the yard next door. He had no sooner
landed when he heard a fierce growl and saw
two big, black eyes glinting in the moonlight.

It was Barker the dog who didn't like cats at all. His mouth was open wide and Catswhiskers could see his big, sharp teeth. In fact, he felt he could see right down into Barker's stomach! Catswhiskers leaped back on to the fence.

"Phew, what a narrow escape," he gasped. "I didn't realize dogs were so unfriendly!"

Catswhiskers was wondering where it might be safe to go when he heard a low, hissing voice him. "Hey, velvet cat," hissed the voice. "What do you think you are doing on *our* patch?"

Catswhiskers turned round to see several of the biggest, meanest-looking cats he had ever set eyes on. Catswhiskers didn't wait a second longer. He simply ran for his life.

Now he was very frightened, and he was also feeling cold and hungry. He wished that he was in the warm in Susie's bedroom with the other toys. Just as he was thinking that the outside world was perhaps a bit *too* exciting, he heard the sound of a van approaching. It suddenly stopped, its glaring headlights shining straight at him. On the side of the van were the words

STRAY CAT CATCHER and a man carrying a big net got out of the van. Catswhiskers decided that it was definitely time to go!

Without thinking about the gangs of sharp-clawed cats or fierce, barking dogs, he ran back home as fast as he could and jumped through the window with great relief.

Snuggled up on the warm bed with all his friends, Catswhiskers decided that perhaps this was the best life for a pajamas case cat after all.

The Chocolate Soldier

A chocolate soldier stood in the window of Mrs Brown's shop. He was particularly proud of his curly chocolate moustache. But best of all he loved his shiny foil uniform with its braid and smart red stripes. He stood to attention on a shelf in the window, staring straight ahead out into the street with chocolate soldiers sugar mice and a twist of liquorice bootlaces.

The summer sun shone through the window of the sweet shop. The chocolate soldier felt pleasantly warm at first, then he started to feel uncomfortably hot. Next he began to feel most peculiar indeed. His chocolate moustache was wilting and his arms were dripping. Before he knew it, he had slipped out through a hole in his silver foil shoe and was pouring off the shelf and out into the street.

THE CHOCOLATE SOLDIER

"Stop! Help!" he shouted, but nobody heard him and, to his horror, he saw he was heading for a stream at the bottom of the street.

"Help me! I can't swim! I'm going to drown!" he cried as he plunged into the running water. But something very strange happened. He looked round and saw that he had a chocolate tail covered in scales and his arms were a pair of fins instead. The cold water had hardened him into the shape of a chocolate fish!

The chocolate soldier was carried downstream, and after a while the stream broadened out into a river. He realized that he would soon be carried out to sea.

"Whatever shall I do?" he wondered. "I'm sure to get eaten by a bigger fish or maybe even a shark!" He tried to swim against the river's flow but the current swept him down river again.

Soon he could see the waves on the shore and then he found himself bobbing up and down on the sea. He saw a boat close by and then he felt a net closing around him. The net tightened and soon he felt himself being hauled out of the water and landed with a "thwack!" on the deck among a pile of fish. The chocolate soldier was relieved when the boat was rowed to the shore.

He thought he would hop over the side, not remembering that he had a fish's tail. But when they reached the shore, he and all the other fish were lifted into a van. The van stopped outside a shop and a man carried the buckets inside, where it smelt of fish, chips and vinegar.

THE CHOCOLATE SOLDIER

The chocolate soldier found himself being lifted up with other fish in a huge metal basket. He saw a terrible sight below. They were heading for a vat of boiling oil! Before they could reach the oil he felt peculiar again. He began to melt and slid through the holes in the basket, into a man's pocket.

The chocolate soldier lay there all day, then the man walked home with the chocolate soldier bouncing up and down. When they arrived at the man's house he felt in his pocket.

"Look I've found a coin," he said to his small son. You can have it – but don't spend it all at once!" he said. The chocolate soldier felt himself being passed from one hand to another.

THE CHOCOLATE SOLDIER

"Now I'm a chocolate coin, and I'm going to be eaten by the boy!" he thought. But he felt himself being slipped into the boy's pocket then bouncing around as the boy ran to a shop. When the chocolate soldier peeped out he saw that he was back in Mrs Brown's sweet shop – the boy was going to try and spend him!

The chocolate soldier called out to his soldier friends in the window, "Pssst! It's me! Help me get out of here!" All the chocolate soldiers could see was a chocolate coin sticking out of the boy's pocket. Then one recognized the voice.

"I've been turned into a coin. Help!" cried the chocolate soldier.

THE CHOCOLATE SOLDIER

"Don't worry, we'll have you out of there in a jiffy!" replied the other soldier.

Quick as a flash, two sugar mice chewed off a length of liquorice bootlace. The soldier lowered it into the boy's pocket, where it stuck to the chocolate coin. The soldiers hauled the coin up onto the shelf. The chocolate soldier's foil uniform was still there on the shelf. All the effort of getting on the shelf had made him warm, and he slipped easily back through the hole in the shoe and into his uniform again.

"I'd like a chocolate soldier," said the boy to Mrs Brown. But when he reached in his pocket the coin had gone.

"Never mind," said kind Mrs Brown, "I'll let you have one anyway." She took down a soldier from the end of the row and gave it to the boy. And as for our chocolate soldier? In the cool of the night he turned back into a smart-looking soldier again.

The Bear and the Ice Kingdom

A king once ruled a sunny, pleasant kingdom with lush forests and meadows, and sparkling rivers. He loved his daughter very much, and she would one day rule the kingdom.

Beyond this was a very different kingdom, an icy-cold place with wind-swept, snowy plains and cold, frozen seas. It was always winter. This kingdom was ruled by a wicked ogre, whose wish was to own the warm lands of his neighbor.

The wicked ogre decided he would kidnap the king's daughter. Then she, like everyone else, would be turned to ice by the cold. When the king died there would be no-one to inherit his kingdom, and the wicked ogre could seize it.

The wicked ogre left his kingdom and went to the king's land disguised as a merchant. When he came to the castle gates he asked if he might show the princess his big bag of wares. She showed him to a room but as soon as she started to look at his goods, the wicked ogre bundled her into the bag and took her off to his kingdom. As soon as the princess felt the cold chill of the wicked ogre's kingdom, she was immediately frozen to ice.

The wicked ogre thought he would just wait for the king to die of old age or a broken heart, then the kingdom would be his. But his evil deed had been seen by one of the king's courtiers. The king sent troops to rescue his daughter, but as soon as they reached the kingdom they, too, were frozen to ice.

There seemed to be no way to get his beloved daughter back, until one day he had an idea. He sent out a royal proclamation saying that anyone who could rescue his daughter would be granted any gift within the king's power.

Many adventurers tried to rescue the king's daughter, but all were turned to ice.

Then one day, the king's dancing bear asked to speak with the king. "I have a plan to rescue your daughter," said the bear.

"And what is your plan?" asked the king.

"It is a secret, your majesty," said the dancing bear. "But I promise to bring her safely home."

The king agreed because after all, every other attempt had failed so what did he have to lose? Travelling by day and night the dancing bear finally reached his destination – a cold, snowy place where his cousin lived. The dancing bear was small and brown, but his cousin was big and white. This bear loved the cold and snow, for he had a thick fur coat. He was a polar bear.

The dancing bear told his cousin the story and the polar bear agreed to rescue the princess. They returned to the king's land, then the polar bear set off on his venture.

When he reached the ogre's ice kingdom a freezing, icy wind blew all around the polar bear, but his thick, warm fur coat kept out the cold. The polar bear finally reached the wicked ogre's castle.

The ogre never expected anyone to be able to enter his kingdom, so he never locked his doors. While he slept in his bedroom, the polar bear searched until he found the frozen princess. He gathered her up, and they were just about to make their escape when the ogre awoke.

As the wicked ogre tried to snatch the princess, the polar bear hit the ogre a mighty blow and the ogre fell down dead. The polar bear carried the princess back to her father's warm kingdom again, and she immediately returned to life.

There was much rejoicing at the return of the king's daughter. The king said to the dancing bear, "You have kept you promise and now I will keep mine. What is your wish?"

"All I ask, your majesty, is that I am freed to roam the forests of your kingdom."

The king immediately granted his wish. And as a reward to the polar bear, he was given the ice kingdom as his own domain which, being so cold, suited him just fine!

Jack and the Beanstalk

Once there was a poor old woman who lived
with her son Jack in a tumble-down cottage by
a pine forest. They were getting poorer as each
winter passed. After one very cruel and cold
winter, the woman turned to her son and said,
"You must take the old brown cow to market
tomorrow and sell her for her meat – she is all
that we have left, so get a good price!"

The next morning Jack took the old brown
cow and started the long journey into town.

Jack had stopped on his way to eat his crust of bread when a farmer passed by. Jack told the farmer where he was heading and why, and the farmer said to Jack, "I'll swap you these dried beans for your old brown cow."

Jack shook his head. "I'm sorry," he said, "but I must take the old brown cow to sell at the market so that my mother and I can buy bread."

The farmer promised Jack that he would make his fortune. Jack finally agreed, and went home with the beans in his pocket.

When he got home his mother cried when Jack told her all they had were dried beans. She snatched the beans from Jack's hand and threw them out of the window in anger.

Jack woke up to discover a huge beanstalk had shot up during the night. He ran downstairs and looked – it disappeared into the clouds. Jack decided to climb the beanstalk.

Jack climbed so high that when he looked down, the tumble-down cottage was a tiny speck far below. Eventually, Jack climbed through the clouds and was amazed when he got to the top to discover another land very different from the one he'd left below.

Everything was HUGE. The grass came up to Jack's shoulder, and in the distance was the largest castle he had ever seen. Jack heard a thunderous rustling in the grass behind him, and he looked round to see a huge giantess towering above him.

"I won't bother to eat you, you're too thin but you might come in handy around the house." said the giantess as she popped Jack in her pocket and carried him into the castle.

She warned Jack not to let her husband, the giant, see him. "He's looking for a boy to pound into bread," she said quite calmly.

The castle shuddered as the giant approached. "Fee Fi Fo Fum," roared the giant. "I smell the blood of an Englishman. Be he alive or be he dead, I'll grind his bones to make my bread."

"Don't be silly," said the giantess, "you never change your socks, it's your feet you can smell."

Satisfied with this answer, the giant sat down and started to count a huge pile of money. Then the giant scooped it all back into the purse, put his feet on the table, and fell asleep.

When the thunderous snores told Jack that it was
safe, he sneaked up on to the table. The purse was
within reach, and Jack dragged it to the edge of
the table and knocked it on to the floor. Jack
dragged the purse to the castle door, down to the
meadow, and down the beanstalk.

When Jack got home with his treasure he showed
it to his mother, who hugged him with joy and
told him not to climb the beanstalk again.

But Jack decided that he would go back to the
castle to find some more treasures. The next
morning before he left the house, he tied a red
scarf around his head, and painted freckles
on his face, so that the giantess would
not recognise him.

Again, the giantess picked Jack up
and popped him into her apron pocket,
and warned him about the terrible giant. Once
more the castle trembled at the giant's approach.

"Fee Fi Fo Fum," roared the giant, "I smell the
blood of an Englishman. Be he alive or be he
dead, I'll grind his bones to make my bread."

"It's your armpits that you can smell," said the
giantess, "because you never wash them."

Satisfied with this answer, the giant sat down
with his hen. Jack saw to his amazement that
the hen had laid a beautiful golden egg!

When Jack heard the giant snoring again, he
sneaked up on to the table and gently took the
hen, then rushed back down the beanstalk.
When Jack returned his mother was waiting for
him, and when Jack showed her the hen, she
hugged him and begged him never to climb
the beanstalk again.

But again, Jack thought about all the
treasures, and the next morning he
climbed the beanstalk all over again.

This time he tied a blue scarf round his head and rubbed dirt into his face, and once again the giantess didn't recognize him. Again she picked Jack up and popped him into her apron pocket, and warned him about the terrible giant. Once more the castle trembled at the giant's approach.

"Fee Fi Fo Fum," roared the giant, "I smell the blood of an Englishman. Be he alive or be he dead, I'll grind his bones to make my bread."

"That'll be the bugs in your hair," said the giantess, "because you never comb it."

This time the giant called for his harp, and when the giant played the strings of the harp, it sang in a beautiful voice. Soon the giant fell asleep and Jack rushed to take the harp, but to his surprise the harp shrieked "Help! Help! I am being stolen."

The giant woke up. Roaring "Fee Fi Fo
Fum,. I smell the blood of an Englishman.
Be he alive or be he dead, I'll grind his bones
to make my bread," he raced after Jack.

Jack began to climb down as quickly as he
could – but the giant wasn't far behind.
When Jack was almost at the bottom he
called for his mother to bring the wood ax,
and then he jumped the rest of the way to the
ground. Jack grabbed the ax and chopped
furiously at the stalk. The giant was almost
down when the beanstalk collapsed on top of
him and he was squashed to nothing.

Jack and his mother never had to worry
about money again.